Walk on the Water

Walk on the Water

W. R. Philbrick

ST. MARTIN'S PRESS

NEW YORK

Design by Dawn Niles

Library of Congress Cataloging-in-Publication Data

Philbrick, W. R. (W. Rodman)
    Walk on the water / W. R. Philbrick.
        p.   cm.
    "A Thomas Dunne book."
    ISBN 0-312-05533-1
    I. Title.
    PS3566.H474W35   1991
    813'.54—dc20   90-15556
                                                                            CIP

First Edition: March 1991

10   9   8   7   6   5   4   3   2   1

For the real Megan Drew

Walk
on
the
Water

Lies, deception, and murder. Basic ingredients. Add a pinch of malice, stir briskly for two or three hundred pages, and you have that concoction called a crime novel.

Sometimes the pot won't stir.

So instead of making mysteries I was snapping rubber bands at a spot on the wall when Meg came home with tears in her eyes. She unlocked the door, kicked off her boots—it was slushing out there—and headed directly to the bedroom, where she lay face down on the bed.

Still cocooned in her puffy green down jacket, I could see that much from my desk. I fidgeted for a few minutes, cleared my throat once or twice, and then resolved that decisive action was required.

What I did was park my chair next to the bed and slip into place beside her with a minimum of fuss.

"February blahs," I said. "And since this is Leap Year and this is the extra day, extra blahs were forecast."

A misty green eye blinked open. "I don't believe it."

I crossed my heart. *"Farmer's Almanac,"* I said. "The almanac is iffy about the weather, but their blah forecast is right on the money."

"They're lying," Meg said, raising herself up. "Fiona would never steal a manuscript."

"Ah," I said. "Fiona. Fiona who?"

"Darling," Meg said in her husky voice.

I closed my eyes, expecting a kiss.

"Fiona Darling," Meg said. "You know, the mystery writer. My big discovery."

*　　*　　*

I made hot cocoa. From the kitchen window the Charles River looked like a skinny gray puddle clotted with patches of dirty ice. The Cambridge skyline was a smudge. Storrow Drive was banked so high with blackened snow the traffic was scarcely visible. Spring looked to be several thousand years away.

"We could do this," I said, sliding a mug along to Meg. "We could go find the sun. I heard it was in the Bahamas somewhere."

"Harold threatened to fire me."

Megan is an editor at Standish House. Harold Standish, the publisher, had inherited the family business. A really terrific squash player, he neither hired nor fired—nor read, from what I could tell.

"He said that?"

Meg wrapped her hands around the mug of cocoa. "'Someone is going to pay for this,' is what he said."

"Has he read Fiona Darling's book?"

Head shake. "He read the letter from Tasha Sturne Holton's law firm. That was enough."

Tasha Sturne Holton. Had a nice ring to it, like the echo of hard cash in a large bank vault. Wife of the late Howard H. Holton, whose New York crime novels featured a tough homicide detective married into a wealthy and powerful family. A family much like the Sturnes, or so it was said. Holton had drowned the previous summer, while surf-casting in Nantucket, and now the widow and her legal posse were claiming that Standish House had published a manuscript stolen from the estate by, it was alleged, Howard Holton's mistress.

"What do you know," I asked, "about Fiona Darling?"

Rumor has it that I used to be on the Boston cops. Not so. I was a civilian working for the Boston Police Department. A lowly tech writer cranking out such classics as *Statistical Evidence of the Barty-Fox Gun Law* and *The Care and Cleaning of the Regulation Holster.* That was days. Nights I prowled the cop bars, collecting the stories I intended to turn into a big novel someday. Someday came unexpectedly one raucous evening when a hotdog vice cop decided to fire off his revolver, missed the floor, and scored a direct hit on my spine.

Depending on how you look at it, it was lucky for me the vice cop was a documented head case. My old pal Finian X. Fitzgerald took his famous mouth into court and convinced the jury that the City of Boston owed me an apartment in a very pricey part of town, a customized van, and the time to write that big novel. That big novel was rejected, very kindly, by Mary Kean, an editor at Standish House. It was Mary who suggested I try my hand at a tightly crafted police procedural. So I did, and eight or nine books later I still do, although some days go better than others, hence my skill at important diversions like rubber band snapping.

"I know she's had some . . . troubles," Meg was saying. "Fiona has certain strange qualities, but she says she was never Howard Holton's mistress and she's certainly not a thief."

"Strange qualities?"

Meg sighed. "She's a creative type, okay? Has a few quirks. Like you."

I ignored that. "What evidence do they have that your quirky Ms. Darling ripped off a story from the late Howard Holton?"

"Nothing solid."

"But?"

"But there are certain . . . resemblances to Holton's style."

"How do you mean?"

"I mean Holton's hero is a homicide cop married into a wealthy Manhattan family. And Fiona's heroine is a homicide detective married to a rich and powerful Boston lawyer."

I waited. "That's it? That similarity is the big literary rip-off?"

"Pretty much. I mean as far as plot goes, I've been told that none of Holton's books use the same plot Fiona used in *Sea Change*."

"You've been *told*? Does that mean you haven't read Howard Holton?"

Meg got up abruptly, rinsed her mug in the sink. Her cheeks were red. Megan Drew blushes when she is either angry or sexually aroused. This was definitely an angry blush.

"That's exactly what Harold Standish said. Like it was a crime I never read Holton's books."

"Holton was good, Meg. One of the best."

Meg turned. "Better than Parker? Better than Mc-Bain? Better than you?"

I hesitated. "It's always difficult to explain, but a writer like Howard Holton, you could recognize his stuff right off, from the very first sentence."

Meg went to the window, drew a wetted finger across the frost. The light was coming in just right, forming a nimbus around her mop of auburn hair. Painting by one of the Dutch masters: *Pretty Woman at the Window*.

"I tried," she said. "I read the reviews. You raved about him. But I was really put off by the tone. He hated women."

"Come on."

"I'm serious. It's subtle, but it's in there—Howard Holton despised women. Look at the detective's family. This horrible shrew of a wife. A daughter who is clearly twisted in some horrible way. A mother-in-law who seems to be based on Medusa."

"Men don't fare much better in his novels, believe me."

"Anyhow, I got halfway into *Top of the Tower* and decided I was quits with Howard Holton. Too many other good novels to read, why waste my time on an author who gave me the creeps?"

You can't argue a person into liking a novel or a novelist. No use trying. I disagreed with Meg's assessment of Holton. Or did I? Had I glossed over an ingrained misogyny in his books? Had I been blinded by an admiration of his skill?

"What does Fiona think?" I asked.

"About what?"

"Holton. Has she read him?"

Meg wet her finger and drew another line on the frost. She was making a triangle. "Fiona thinks he's great. Says he was obviously a sick man, but with a wonderful talent for narrative. That's a quote. Admits she was inspired by him."

"By him or his books?"

"Both. Met him at a book signing at The Raven's Nest a couple of years ago. Told the great man she was working on a mystery, he was very encouraging."

"She had an affair with him?"

Meg hesitated. "She says no."

"And he didn't give her one of his unpublished manuscripts?"

Meg shook her head. "Uh-uh. But you know what really bugs me?"

I waited until she drew the third line, completing the triangle. More of a frost pyramid, really.

"Fiona won't defend herself. Says she *tried* to write like Howard goddamned Holton."

Meg went out to buy fresh pasta while I worked up a pesto sauce. It was a variation on Meg's recipe—I used two cloves of garlic instead of one. And walnuts instead of pine nuts—Meg always says walnuts are nuttier and I always say you should know, you nut; a good pesto requires banter as well as fresh basil. Or as close as you can come to fresh in Boston on the twenty-ninth day of February.

I won't mention here my ritual joke about extra virgin olive oil.

The dinner guests arrived separately. First it was Finian X. Fitzgerald, who would be treating pasta, salad, and bread as a mere appetizer to the meat and potatoes his wife Lois would dutifully dole out when he arrived home. Fitzy helped himself to a beer, stripped off his necktie, and gave out his deepest Hibernian sigh.

"I have been cut and wounded, comrades," he said, running a hand through his thinning red hair. "Kicked when I was down. Spat on by lemon suckers."

Meg, watching the water boil, said, "You lost a case?"

Fitzy looked wounded. A big, pink-faced bear with a spear in his side. "Bite your tongue. I lost a *motion.* Doesn't mean I lost a case. Lose a case, I wouldn't be dropping by sober. Lose a case, hey, they carry me out on my shield."

"I hope 'they' is six strong men," Meg said.

"Glad to see marriage hasn't softened your edge, Megan darling."

I ceased tossing the salad and put down the wooden tongs. "Be nice, both of you. Meg, our friend Fitzy has had a rough day. And Fitzy, our friend Megan has also had a rough day."

"Hence the invitation for free legal advice."

"Not free," I said, putting the plates out. "You'll be well compensated with garlic. If that doesn't seem fair, send us the bill."

Fitzy put his hands up, surrendering. "Ease up, kids. A mere jest. Like I said, what little I know about this particular subject I'll give you free. Might bill you for a breath mint. And Meg? If Mr. Racquetball fires you without due cause, I'll sue his ass from here to the Myopia Hunt Club, that's a promise."

"Squash," I said. "Harold plays squash."

"Whatever."

He got up, helped himself to another beer, and gave Meg a nudge on his way back to the stool. She swiped at him with a wooden spoon and was careful to miss.

Fitzy twisted off the bottle cap and said: "One small question I got, before the other party arrives. Any possibility that the accused came into possession of an unpublished Holton manuscript and put her name on the title page after he died? I mean, any chance she actually did it?"

The doorbell rang.

"We'll ask her," I said.

3

'd never had the pleasure. Fiona Darling entered carrying two bottles, one of red wine and the other of soda water. Ash blonde hair cut in pageboy bangs that didn't quite fit with her sorrowful brown eyes. Face somewhat drawn and puffy, as if she'd been crying. That careful job of makeup that a woman of forty shows to the world. Slim, but with a way of carrying herself that suggested a weight problem in the past.

"J. D. Hawkins," she said, handing me the wine. "I recognize you from your dust jackets."

"Jack," I said. "How do you do, Fiona?"

"I've been better."

Fitzy put down his beer, dried his hands, and greeted her. "I'm the mouthpiece," he said.

"My pleasure," Fiona said.

"Don't be silly," Fitzy said with a grin. "Not under the circumstances, it can't be. Let's just see if we can get through this, shall we?"

Megan's rule is eat first and then conduct business over coffee. Fitzy isn't very good with other people's rules. He started in as the wine was being poured—soda for Fiona Darling, who did not drink, or who no longer drank, the distinction wasn't clear to me.

"First thing," he said, pointing at himself with a breadstick. "I'm a friend of the family, so if I ask an insulting question, feel free to throw something at me. Preferably something soft or wet, because I'm a bleeder."

"I'll try to restrain myself," Fiona said dryly.

I started to like her right about then. It takes a certain inner confidence to stand up to Finian X. Fitzgerald. Instinct told me that if she could hold her own with my old friend she wasn't the type to steal another writer's stuff.

"Okay," Fitzy said. "Here goes. First, crux of the accusation we get from the firm representing the late Howard Holton and his heirs: The novel you claim as yours was written by Mr. Holton, and therefore owned by his estate. The inference that you had a romantic relationship with Mr. Holton is used to bolster the accusation."

Fiona carefully buttered her bread and ate it in small bites. "She's crazy," she said.

"Excuse me?"

"Tasha. Mrs. Holton. She's nuts."

Fitzy grimaced. "I see. Do you happen to know the lady?"

Fiona shook her head. "Heard it from someone who does."

"So there's no truth to the assertion?"

"I was never Howard's mistress. I never stole anything from anyone. I wrote the book, it's mine."

Fitzy gave her the kind of eyeball usually reserved for the victims of his cross-examinations. She did not blink.

"Glad to hear it," he said, nodding as if satisfied. "Advising guilty clients can be fun, but it gives me gas. Plea bargain and take a bicarb, that's my motto. Innocent is easier on the guts, and I always take it to trial. Not that I'd be the best guy to represent you if, God forbid, it comes to that. You'll want a specialist in copyright law. I could recommend one or two."

Fiona shook her head quickly. "All that's happened so far is the letter. If somebody can convince these people they've made a mistake, they'll drop the whole thing. Lawsuits are expensive, right?"

"Very," Fitzy said, twisting his fork into the pasta. "On the other hand, the Sturne family is loaded. Luxury hotels. One right here in Boston. And Stanford and Davies is a great big Fifth Avenue law firm. No doubt the Sturnes have them on retainer."

Fiona's tone of voice was soft and husky. You had to listen carefully to hear the restrained anger, the fist in her throat. "But why should they hound me? *Sea Change* has gotten good reviews, but Megan says I'll be lucky to earn ten thousand dollars on the hardcover edition. Chicken feed to those people."

Fitzy was alternating between sips of red wine and beer. No wonder he sometimes needed a bicarb. He gave us his best Celtic shrug, the weight of centuries of whiskey, wisdom, and doomed poetry heavy on his shoulders. Spencer Tracy before his hair went white. "All kinds of reasons for threatening lawsuits. Not always money, contrary to popular opinion. Some lawsuits are about dueling for honor, or exacting revenge, or going to war."

Fiona nodded. She hadn't touched her salad or pasta. The glass of soda was empty. "They don't know me," she said. "I'm a stranger. No reason for revenge or war."

He opened his hands. "A big firm like Stanford and Davies doesn't go *looking* for potential lawsuits, especially not those that are hard to win—and disputes over copyright can take years to settle. My guess is they're responding to the Widow Holton. Putting the gears in motion at her insistence. Maybe she's consumed with grief. Convinced that any work similar to her husband's must have been appropriated."

Fiona had her hands folded. I could see the knuckles going white. She sighed, looked down at her untouched plate. "I might have known," she said. "It was too good to be true. After all these years of trying I finally publish a novel and now somebody I don't even know is trying to spoil it for me. And you're saying they're rich and powerful enough to make it stick."

"I'm saying no such thing," Fitzy said.

"Let's face facts, Mr. Fitzgerald. I'm not wealthy. I can't fight this on my own. And my contract states that the author is solely responsible for the contents. The publisher provides legal representation only at his option."

"Ouch." Fitzy winced. "That's in your contract?"

"I was told it was more or less standard."

"Less," Fitzy said, "but pretty typical. Publishers tend to hyperventilate at the thought of long, expensive lawsuits. Harold Standish is more cautious than most. He'd never risk the family business over defending one book—or one author, for that matter."

"So I'm on my own."

Fitzy nodded, finished his beer.

"This seems really unfair," Meg said.

"It is," Fitzy agreed. "I've got one piece of advice and you can have it for free."

"Yes?"

"Head 'em off at the pass."

After Fitzy left, Fiona Darling seemed to sink inside herself. She was smaller, older, aware of forces beyond her control. I busied myself in the kitchen, loading the dishwasher, making fresh coffee, while Meg did her woman-to-woman thing. I could hear the low sibilation of their intermingled voices without being able to distinguish words.

After a while Meg strolled into the kitchen and said, "Hiding are we?"

"You know how I get if a woman cries."

"Come on," she said, giving me a quick kiss. "Tears are over. We've decided to fight."

Fiona was standing by the sliding glass door, staring down at the glowing insect trails of headlights in the snowbound trough of Storrow Drive. On the distant shore of the dark river the moon was reflecting cold and pale off the MIT dome. A pretty scene, easily mistaken for tranquillity.

"I'm a writer," she said without turning from the glass. "I have to write. If I'm going to live, I need to publish. Therefore Tasha Sturne Holton has to be convinced that she is mistaken. Her dead husband didn't write *Sea Change*. I did."

Fiona's novel had been on the nightstand for several weeks. A getting-around-to-it book. While Meg watched *Casablanca* with the sound down—she knew all the lines by heart—I cracked open *Sea Change* and was drawn into the story by the very first sentence:

She walked off the boat in her bare feet, holding one shoe, and never looked back at the place where she had watched him drown.

Three hundred and ten pages later the other shoe finally dropped in that satisfying it-had-to-end-like-this finality that indicates a story well told. I closed the book, put it back on the stand, and turned to Megan.

She was lying on her back, mouth slightly open, unwillingly asleep. Bogart had long since watched Ingrid fly off into the fog. The hell with it. I nudged her awake.

"I read it."

"Huh?"

"Fiona's book. Terrific stuff."

Meg surfaced. "Liked it?"

"Damn good," I said. "She's got a voice of her own."

"So," she said, rolling over. "You believe her now?"

"Yes," I said.

Moments later Meg was back under. I slipped my arms around her but sleep did not come easy. I kept thinking about Fiona Darling and her book. One thing bothered me. She was as good as Howard Holton, maybe better.

And I was jealous.

4

The Raven's Nest is on Mass. Ave. in Cambridge, in the stretch between Harvard Square and Central Square. The sign suspended over the sidewalk is supposed to be a large black bird, of the species who quoth "nevermore." It looks more like a bat of the flying rat species.

I happened to mention this to Lynda Raven one time and she refused to speak to me for weeks. She threatened to take my books off the shelf—how dare I denigrate a sign carved by her brother the sculptor—but a friend told me she never actually ditched my books because that would have deprived her of the chance to lambaste me whenever a customer bought a Detective Casey novel. I made up to her with a stuffed raven perched on a plaster bust of Pallas. Lynda, of course, put it above the door and we've been on cautious terms ever since.

Ms. Raven has a certain way about her. Offered as evidence, a sign posted in the six-slot parking lot adjacent to her building:

RAVEN'S NEST CUSTOMERS ONLY
ALL OTHERS DETONATED

In lieu of detonation or towing (which in Cambridge often amounts to the same thing) Lynda sometimes lets the air out of all four tires and/or scrawls ILLITERATE SCUM on the windshield with a special brand of irremovable lipstick she keeps for that purpose. Legend has it that a customer from the nearby pub, The Plough and Stars, having discovered his vehicle in just such a sad and deflated state, went into the store to confront the owner and emerged with his toes stomped on and the same words neatly lettered on his forehead.

Well, maybe. Personally I've never seen anyone with a forehead wide enough to accommodate ILLITERATE SCUM, not even at The Plough.

The gentle proprietor was behind the counter when I rolled in.

"Door please!"

I swung around, pushed the door shut as Lynda climbed down off her laddered stool. Seated in my chair I'm still an inch or two taller—Lynda claims to be four foot six. Maybe in heels. Don't call her a midget, though. Heaven knows what might end up on your forehead.

"Megan called me," she said. "What a load of hornswoggle."

"Wouldn't know," I said. "What is hornswoggle, exactly?"

"Stuff that comes out of a lawyer's mouth."

"Ah," I said. "Of course."

"Tea?"

I nodded. Free tea for the browsers at The Raven's Nest. That and a mammoth collection of crime genre books compensate for the proprietor's occasional outbursts, as in "Buy it or begone!" if she catches you smudging a page. Welcome to read, mind you, just beware of smudging, a high crime on this end of Massachusetts Avenue.

"Back room," she said, handing me a cup and saucer.

I followed her into the back room, set the cup and saucer on a stack of book cartons. "So you're a pal of Fiona Darling's," I said. "Is that right?"

I should mention that although diminutive in stature, Lynda is perfectly proportioned, with a fine figure, porcelain features, and lovely, snapping brown eyes. She snapped them at me and said, "I'm nobody's 'pal,' Jack. What a rotten word that is. Almost as repulsive as 'chum.' You know what chum is? The little fish they grind up to feed to bigger fish."

I sighed. Conversing with Lynda can be like defusing a very tricky time bomb, each ill-chosen word a tick in the wrong direction.

"But you know her, right?" I said. "She stayed here for a while?"

"Rented a room."

Lynda's building is a two-and-a-half-story job: the Nest on ground level, her apartment on the second floor, and a garret that had been converted into rooms, ostensibly for a bed and breakfast. Lynda soon discovered that B & B customers were rather fussy—they wanted the breakfast part, too, and preparing it was, as she put it, "a royal pain in the gut." Now the rooms were occasionally let to writers. Suspicion is that Lynda "forgets" to collect the rent if the writer is without funds, a generosity she would rudely deny if you dared to ask—and you don't, believe me.

"But she wrote *Sea Change* while she was here, do I have that right?" I said.

"Correct," she said. "Ten weeks, day and night."

"I notice she dedicated it to you. 'For Lynda, who sheltered me from the storm.'"

"I hate author dedications," Lynda said. "Only things worse are those wretched dust jacket bios. 'Mr Hawkins resides in Boston, scene of his crimes.' Too goddamn cute."

"I wrote that," I said.

"Of course you did. Authors always write their dust jacket bios. In the third person, too. I never trust people who speak about themselves in the third person. That includes Wade Boggs and Henry Kissinger."

I sighed. We'd had this conversation, or a variation of it, before.

"She wrote the book," Lynda said. "I'll swear to it in court."

"You *saw* her writing it?"

"Well, I wasn't standing over her shoulder, was I? But I could hear that damn printer spitting out pages every night."

"Ah, well, that's not the same thing, is it?" I said, and got ready to duck.

Lynda made a face, crossed her slender arms. "Listen to me, Jack. I know writers and I know fakers. You should hear some of the bogus stuff that comes in off the street. Telling me they've got this great idea for a book, it wasn't the butler did it, it was the maid? Or how about a coke addict sleuth who plays the violin? And believe me, Fiona isn't one of *that* bunch. We talked about *Sea Change* before she sat down to write it. I saw it evolve. Fiona's the real thing, a novelist in her guts."

"*Sea Change* is a fine novel. If she wrote it."

"Well take it from me—she did. And if she keeps it up, Fiona will be right up there, as good as Robert B. Parker or even Howard Holton, and that's pretty damn good."

I drank the cooling tea, considered how fierce were the women defending Fiona Darling's integrity. Megan had been no less convinced of her talent. Odd that Fiona herself seemed to have less passion on the subject. Was it because she felt herself to be a protégée of the late Howard Holton? In his debt for a kind of vision, a way of looking at a story, if not for the story itself?

I asked Lynda how well she had known Holton.

She gave me a stony look. "Wasn't exactly your social butterfly type," she said. "I knew him a little."

"He did book signings here."

"If it was convenient. If he happened to be in the Boston area."

"And that's how Fiona met him?"

"I assume it is. He had quite a following. Lots of fans turned out. I assume Fiona met him the usual way, by asking him to sign one of his books."

I nodded. "I thought his following was pretty much male."

Lynda shook her head. "About half and half, I'd say. Some women find him sexist, others found him . . . interesting."

"And Fiona admired the author as well as his books?"

"You'd have to ask her. And if you're trying to suggest he made a pass at Fiona, forget it."

"How can you be so sure?" I asked.

"Look. As a writer Howard Holton was top of the heap, right up there with Chandler. As a man he was a chauvinist pig. Liked his women young and doe-eyed. Any female over the age of twenty-five would have to settle for taking the book to bed, not the author. You want to know about Howard? Sober he was okay. Put a few drinks into him and he was a mean-tempered son of a bitch."

I'd heard as much, and not only from Megan. Holton had a reputation as a feisty skirt chaser who displayed little of the sensitivity of the world-weary police detective he wrote about. Brawler, womanizer, and a really terrific prose stylist. The kind of intense, two-fisted writer that H. L. Mencken called a "bourbon genius."

A chime sounded, indicating that a customer had entered the store.

"So," I said. "How is *Sea Change* selling?"

"Hotcakes," Lynda said.

I was surprised. Standish House, ever cautious with an unknown author, had ordered a small printing, no publicity, no tour.

Lynda gave me a grim smile. "The rumors are already flying, Jack. My customers are pretty sophisticated about these things. They know there may not be a second edition."

5

There are several ways to complete the Boston-Manhattan connection. You can take one of Mr. Trump's airplanes, with the *faux* marble sinks that are supposed to make you feel entrepreneurish when you wash your hands at thirty thousand feet. You can gamble that Amtrak, the bus on rails, will not break down in New Haven. Or you can do it the American way, on wheels of your own. I find the latter the least trouble and often the quickest— less than four hours door to door, and without the hassle of navigating through Newark Airport or Penn Station in a wheelchair.

Megan had come along for moral support, and for the chance to call me a Boston driver, from my point of view not an insult.

"Well, he *did* get out of the way, didn't he?" I said when we were safely inside the Sturne Royal Hotel underground parking facility on Central Park South.

"But you almost killed him," Megan said. "An innocent pedestrian."

"No pedestrian is innocent when he's pushing a rack of suits against red lights in the garment district," I said. "Urban traffic is a horror show. The way it works best for all concerned, I play psycho-driver, the pedestrian plays Norman Bates out for a stroll. And we both give a good performance."

We'd gone down to New York on Fitzy's advice, to try to head Tasha Sturne Holton off at the pass. To reason with her. Mrs. Holton had agreed to allot us fifteen minutes of her undivided attention, with a lawyer present.

"I still think Fiona should have come along," I said, rolling for the elevators.

"You just don't understand," Megan said, "how vulnerable she feels about all this. How *assaulted*. Also, she's working on her next book."

I let it go. I was supposed to be working on a book, too, and this was in the nature of an interesting distraction. Better than shooting elastic bands at the wall, or vegging out on MTV.

We were early for the appointment and killed thirty minutes in the Sturne Royal lobby. Megan felt underdressed in her sensible down parka. "I always wondered where all those dead animals went," she said, watching a floor-length white fox saunter by on spike heels.

"A white fox is not exactly road kill."

"No indeed."

"Would you have any objection to wearing a mink coat?"

Megan grinned. "Is that an offer?"

"Theoretical question," I said uneasily—there was a furrier within spitting distance.

"Theoretical answer? Until I give up eating meat I have no objection to ranch-raised mink. But skip the white fox if it died in a trap, in agony."

"That sounds like a compromise," I said.

"It is," Meg said. "How about a teensie-weensie mink hat?"

"Wouldn't go with the parka," I said.

"Then start at the top and work down."

We escaped from the lobby without having to leg-trap a credit manager. Before being allowed to board the private penthouse elevator, we waited for the operator to confirm our appointment. Beasley—that was the name engraved on his uniform tag—studiously avoided noticing Megan's parka and jeans outfit, or my scruffy bomber jacket, or my chair. But by the time the lift reached the penthouse I felt several dozen stories above my station.

"Do we ring for Jeeves?" I asked as the doors slid open.

"Please wait in the foyer," Beasley advised. "You're expected."

There was nothing *faux* about the marble in the foyer, or the brass inlay, or the pale roses in the tall vases. You expected a perfect little girl to emerge from behind the vase pedestal, dressed and coiffed for a family portrait by John Singer Sargent.

"I could live here," I said. "Just in the foyer. Let 'em keep the rest of the place, I wouldn't want to dust it."

"I just hope they don't make us leave by the back stairs," Meg said.

A few minutes later one of the massive paneled doors opened.

"Mr. Hawkins?"

No doubt she was penthouse staff, but the posture was pure flight attendant. As we were led inside, I caught a glimpse of a sheer glass wall with a spectacular view of Central Park before we were diverted into another marble hallway.

"Tasha will see you in her office," our guide informed us. "She's quite busy today, so I'm afraid the fifteen minute allotment cannot be exceeded."

I swallowed a wise remark about quality time— sometimes the best way to get even is by leaving wheel marks on priceless Persian carpets.

Tasha's office was relatively cozy, with paneled walls, a working fireplace, and drapes drawn back to show off a slightly different, though equally spectacular view of the park. From this vantage point the city looked to be a manicured winter forest enclosed by a border of toylike buildings. Far below, tiny hackney carriages inched along loops through the park. The scene was as beautiful and distant and as strangely artificial as a snow scene in a water-filled glass globe.

"I'm Tasha Sturne Holton," she said, coming out of the light to offer a thin, cool hand. "This is Mr. Thurston Breen, Jr., an attorney with Stanford and Davies."

Tasha was a long-legged woman of extreme, horsey slenderness. Dark-eyed, with lacquer-black hair worn in short bangs, and so many large white teeth that her lips were never entirely closed, she had the kind of fragile beauty that might, with a slight change of expression, become weirdly repulsive. "Is this your attorney, Mr. Hawkins?" she said, indicating Megan.

I made the introduction and said, "Ms. Drew is an editor with Standish House."

"I bought *Sea Change* from Fiona Darling," Meg explained.

"Oh." Turning to her attorney, who was standing by a leather wingback near the fireplace, she said, "Thurston, how should we handle this?"

Thurston, who had the medium height and rangy build of a shortstop, blinked his mild blue eyes and waved Megan to a seat. "I think Mrs. Holton had the impression you'd have an attorney present, Mr. Hawkins."

"Didn't know I needed one," I said. "Mrs. Holton isn't suing me, that I know of, and I've no reason to sue her."

Thurston chuckled. With his small pink lips pursed he had the face of a highly intelligent cherub. Thirty or so, and adhering to the attorney's dress code that mandates dark blue pinstripes, rep tie, and elegant black wingtips. I made a small wager with myself that he wore galoshes on a regular basis.

"Has Ms. Darling retained an attorney?" he asked.

I shook my head. "We're hoping that won't be necessary. We think, Megan and I, that there's been a misunderstanding. All we want is a chance to—"

The attorney held up his hand, stopping me. "I'm afraid there has been a misunderstanding. When Mr. Fitzgerald contacted our firm, we formed the impression Ms. Darling was ready to make a deal, and that you were acting as emissary."

"Deal?"

He nodded. "Something along the lines of withdrawing the book from publication and returning the copyright to the estate of Howard Holton. At which point Tasha would be willing to let the matter drop."

"Tell them to go away, please," Tasha said. She stood facing the big window, a thin silhouette in a glare of winter light.

I glanced at my watch. "We've got twelve minutes, Mr. Breen. Would you care to hear what I have to say?"

"This is not a productive meeting," he said pleasantly. "It would be better to cut it off now. Sorry about the misunderstanding."

Megan said, "This really sucks, you know that? We drive a couple of hundred miles for a lousy fifteen minutes and then you won't even listen to us."

"So sorry to have offended you, Ms. Drew. But I'm afraid neither of you have legal authority in this matter. You are, in a purely technical sense, interlopers."

"I'm her editor, damn it," Meg said, standing up. "I bought the book and I damn well know that Fiona wrote it. And now I'm supposed to get out of the way because some anorexic society bitch with a pet lawyer wants to ruin an innocent woman?"

I'll give this much to Thurston Breen, Jr., he never lost his cool, not even in the presence of Megan Drew in full temper. "I'm sorry, but there's really no point in continuing along this line."

"Come on, Meg," I said. "This isn't working."

Megan, blushing in anger, tried to make Tasha face her. "You afraid to look us in the eye, Mrs. Holton? Just tell me this—what do you expect to get out of Fiona? You don't even *know* the woman."

"Thurston!" It came out as a strangled shriek. Tasha holding herself rigid, keeping her face to the window.

Banished to the marble foyer, the big door locked behind us, we waited for Beasley to bring up the elevator.

Megan gritted her teeth. "Of all the nerve."

"Beautiful view, though," I said. "Do you think it's rent controlled?"

Megan allowed as how she wasn't in the mood for light banter. She suggested I put a lid on it.

"Consider it lidded," I said, and shut up.

We waited. No doubt we were being punished for rattling the bars on Tasha's gilded cage.

"Hssssst. Hssssst."

The echoes in the foyer made it hard to pinpoint the source of the hissing. Finally one of the smaller doors opened wide enough to show us a glimpse of a tall, plump boy wearing a black silk bathrobe. He hissed again, motioning to us.

"In here," he whispered. "This could be *fun.*"

6

The plump boy in the black silk robe was Brant Allan Sturne, age twenty-three. His feet were bare and I couldn't help noticing that he had six toes on his left foot. He saw me noticing and said, "Pretty weird, huh? Runs in the family. Tasha had hers removed, but I think it's creepy to have things cut off your own body, don't you?"

Brant had a two-room suite all to himself. Bedroom, playroom, adjoining bath. He had invited us into the playroom, which looked as if it had been converted from a library. It had high ceilings and high windows that were shuttered with thick drapes, so that only a few knife blades of daylight penetrated the gloom. There were still bookshelves along one wall, although most of the books had been replaced by hundreds of videocassette boxes. A large rear-projection television seemed to be the central toy, surrounded by video games, arcade machines, some sort of torture device by Nautilus, and one very odd touch—a life-size inflatable doll, of the type sold in joke or porno shops. It had been filled with helium and floated feet up, head tethered by a velvet noose to the Nautilus machine.

"That's Trixie," Brant said with a smirk, not the least embarrassed. "Left over from my birthday party. You know, instead of balloons?"

"You're Tasha's brother?" I asked.

"The one and only. So tell me, I'm dying to know, are you Howie's friends from Boston?"

When I explained who we were and why we had come to see his sister, he seemed only slightly disappointed. "Oh I *heard* about that," he said. "Haven't had a chance to read the book yet. Did Howie really write it and give it to the girl?"

"If you mean Fiona Darling, no, we don't think he did. We think she wrote it herself."

Megan perched, rather gingerly, on the arm of an upholstered chair. Brant flopped down on an exercise mat and folded his hands behind his head. He was handsome enough, in a fleshy kind of way, with a prominent chin and Tasha's long-lashed dark eyes. I got the impression that he didn't think of us as real. We were new and rather interesting components of a game his big sister had thrown out into the foyer, and now it was his turn to play.

"Tasha's so bee-oot-ifull," he said, gazing languidly up at the high ceiling. "Beautiful but twisted. Twisted sister, da dum, da dee. I think I know what this is all about. This is all about being mad at Howie."

"But Howard Holton is dead," Meg pointed out.

Brant closed his eyes and smiled. He looked very comfortable, stretched out on the mat. As if content to stay in his playground suite forever, no need to venture out into the real world. "What difference does dead make?" he said. "If he *is* dead, I mean."

"Why would there be any doubt?"

Brant's eyes blinked open. "There's always doubt when there's no body, right?" Seeing my expression he cranked himself up on one elbow and said, "You mean you didn't *know*?"

He seemed delighted at my ignorance.

I glanced at Megan, who shrugged. "I know he drowned," I said. "I guess I assumed the body was recovered."

"Nope," Brant said with obvious satisfaction. "Vanished. Down the big drain. Into thin air, except it wasn't the air it was the ocean. Can you say 'vanished into the thin ocean'? Because that's what Howie did."

"But there were witnesses," Megan pointed out.

"Oh yes," Brant said, flopping down again. "Several convenient witnesses. Geeks he picked up in some low-rent bar in the Village. All there to watch the mighty Howie land a fish. I heard when it happened they got so *upset,* these Howie friends, that they drank all the Howie liquor."

"These friends have names?"

Brant giggled. "Know what? You sound sort of like Howie. He liked to talk that way sometimes—tough-guy talk."

"Brant, I'm not trying to be a tough guy. But it would be very helpful to us if we could talk with a few of Holton's intimate friends."

As Brant cocked a foot up over his knee the robe dropped away, making his lack of pajamas very obvious. Megan, sitting in the line of fire, so to speak, got up and moved to the video storage shelves, pretending to study the titles.

"I guess it depends on what you mean by intimate," Brant said. "Howie knew *everybody* but nobody knew Howie. Not really. He was the original Mr. Cool. He and Tasha got married when I was eight years old, right? And I figured, wow, this neat guy is going to be my big brother. But it never happened."

"You didn't get along?"

Brant made a face. "We got along fine. Howie really *was* pretty cool. It's just, you know, the big brother type of thing never happened."

Megan looked at me and rolled her eyes.

"Brant," she said. "A couple of minutes ago you asked if we were Howie's friends from Boston. Did he *have* friends in Boston?"

A sly grin from Brant, who had dropped his feet, tucked the robe around his legs. "One at least. A woman-type friend."

"You mean a girlfriend?"

"I assume. There wasn't any other kind, not for Howie. For a while he was doing Boston almost every week. Told Tasha he was researching a book. A 'true crime' book, he said." Brant smirked, flapped his long-lashed eyes. "Well, use your imagination. Adultery is a true crime, right? Or at least *some* people think it is."

"Your sister, for instance?"

Brant got up from the exercise mat, swaying slightly. "Buzz time," he said, opening a small re-frigerator built into the wall. "Wine cooler?" he asked me, holding out a bottle. "How about you?" he asked Megan.

We both declined. He drank straight from the bottle, made a halfhearted attempt to stifle a burp. You could see where his eyes changed almost imme-diately, a glaze of inner distance.

"Fucking around," he said. "Nah, that never both-ered Tasha. Putting us in his books, *that's* what Tasha hated. Personally, I thought it was sort of cool, even if he did make me a stepdaughter instead of a brother-in-law. At least Tasha got to stay his wife, even if he made her older and, you know, more weird or what-ever."

"He admitted the character in his books was based on you?"

Brant nodded. "Sure. Only he said it wasn't *really* me, which is pretty obvious since I'm not a girl and I'm not gay, even if you *think* I'm gay, which a lot of people do for some reason. Do you?"

"Do I what?" I said, uneasy.

"Think I'm gay."

"But you just said you weren't."

"Yes, yes," he said impatiently, "but never mind what I just said. Did you assume I was gay? I don't mind if you did, I just want to know. I'm sort of like taking a survey."

"Then yes, I guess I assumed you were gay."

Brant drained the bottle, went to the refrigerator and withdrew another. "Tell me why, please. Was it my beautiful eyes? The way I talk? My, uh, robe?" he said, turning quickly so the robe twirled like a dress, exposing his bare legs.

"I didn't really think about it," I said. "Not until you asked."

He sighed. My answer was rather disappointing. He turned to Megan. "How about you, darling? Think I was gay?"

Megan shook her head and said, "You're putting on an act. You want people to wonder about your sexuality. It gives you a kick."

Brant coughed. A little fizz of the wine cooler came out his nose and he had to stop and find a tissue. After he'd quit coughing he dropped the tissue to the floor and embraced a reluctant Megan.

"Oh, you *do* understand. Why this is fabulous. *You're* fabulous. And you put it so nicely. Most people, when I first meet them, just assume I'm kinky and perverted. Which, of course, I am—but there's a lot more to it than that. I suppose you and him"—he indicated me—"you have some kind of *thing* going?"

"We're married."

"Really?" He pulled away from Meg, looked at both of us. "That's nice. Really nice. Is it fun being married?"

He seemed sincere, as if he thought it possible that marriage was a kind of game, just another means of extracting pleasure. In the world of penthouse-on-the-park, maybe that was a legitimate conclusion.

Brant was about to ask another question when a telephone rang. He grinned impishly. "Bet I know who *that* is," he said. The phone was near the refrigerator, another opportunity to supply himself with a fresh wine cooler. "Why Tasha, what a surprise," he crooned into the receiver. "I was just thinking about you. What?

Slow down, what are you talking about? But how could you lose a man in a wheelchair, Tasha? It doesn't make sense. Oh. Yeah, sure. Well, how should *I* know, maybe the Beezer *did* take them down and he doesn't remember. All that going up and down in the elevator causes brain damage or something. Get Thurston to check with the lobby. *Ciao.*"

He hung up, returned to his exercise mat, and assumed a kind of lotus position, a big smile illuminating his handsome, man-boy face. "Poor Tasha, she's *so* excitable. And I think she suspects I kidnapped you. Of course she can't come in and look because that would be against the rules. And if she sends Thurston in, she *knows* I'd do something naughty to him. Pull his tie or maybe flash him. You did meet Thurston?"

I said we'd had the pleasure.

"Oh please," Brant said. "You can't mean pleasure, not with Thurston. I said to Tasha, I'll bet you that man has a zipper on his boxer shorts, just to be sure he's never *exposed.*"

"I think we'd better go," I suggested.

"But we're just starting to have *fun,*" he said, pouting. "Pay no attention to Tasha or that filthy lawyer. Don't you just hate lawyers?"

"Brant," I said. "How did your sister happen to read *Sea Change?*"

"What change?"

"Fiona Darling's novel. The book your sister apparently thinks was written by Howard Holton."

"Did you ask her?"

"Never got the chance," I said. "Is Tasha a big reader? I mean does she read lots of mysteries? Follow the reviews, that sort of thing?"

Brant scoffed. "Tash? Are you serious? Not unless it has lots of pretty pictures, preferably of her. Howie used to get mad because she never read *his* books, her own husband. Tasha likes to have things done for her, books are too much like work. Which, I have to admit, I'm pretty much the same way. It's easier to wait for the movie. Except, you know, none of Howie's books ever got to be movies."

"Why was that?" I asked, knowing full well that most novels are never made into movies, but Holton's popular series, with its atmosphere of greed and corruption in high society, had seemed a natural for dramatization.

Brant grinned, clicked his perfect white teeth. "Think about it. You're a movie producer. Do you want to risk a lawsuit by Sturne International?"

"You'd have threatened to sue your own brother-in-law?"

Brant put a hand over his heart. "Not *me*. I'd *love* to see all of us in a movie. What a delicious idea."

"Your sister, then," Megan said. "But if she hated the books so much, why didn't she try to do something about it sooner? Why wait until Holton was dead?"

Brant lay back and closed his eyes. He looked almost beatific, there on the mat, with his bare ankles crossed. "Don't get the wrong idea about Tasha. She doesn't like lawyers any better than I do. When my parents died we got turned over to the trust lawyers. They ran everything until Tasha turned twenty-one. She'd never sue her own husband, not when he lived here with us, and she wouldn't be thinking about it now if she thought he was really dead."

"Tasha thinks her husband faked his own death?" Meg said. "The drowning was a phony?"

"Why not?" Brant said. "I told you he was a cool guy."

7

C all it *Escape From the Sturne Royal* and shoot it tight, so you can see the sweat on the brow of Beasley the elevator operator, trapped in the escape conspiracy by the fiendish man-boy Brant Sturne. Who rode all the way to the lobby with us, still dressed in his black silk robe.

Cut to his bare feet, the ominous sixth toe. Flavor with eerie synthesizer sound effects: *dum da dc dum dweee . . .*

Quick cut to Thurston Breen, Jr., checking with security guards in the lobby. Will he turn in time to see the beautiful woman with the auburn hair slip away, accompanied by a menacing individual in a wheel-chair?

Will he see Brant Sturne wave bye-bye as the ele-vator doors slide shut?

Quickcut to a van trapped in gridlock traffic on Central Park South.

"You know the only thing missing?" Megan was saying. "The room with padded walls. Hell, the whole penthouse should have been padded. What a crazy family."

"It's all that money," I said, inching the van through a clotted intersection. "After three or four generations of inbreeding with other trust funds, the gene pool is depleted. Result, Brant and Tasha."

"I sort of liked Brant," Meg said. "I feel sorry for him."

"Sorry? The boy is worth umpteen millions. The world is his oyster."

"So why is he hiding in that awful room and watch-ing sick videos?"

I remembered that Megan had been perusing the cassette collection. "What kind of sick?" I asked.

"Snuff movies. A preoccupation with hanging, strangulation, and self-abuse."

"Self-abuse?"

"I'd call it that, if you do it while watching pictures of dead people, or people pretending to be dead."

"You're right," I said. "Poor Brant."

We had booked a reservation at the Gramercy Park Hotel, and made it there in just under an hour— not bad for thirty-five blocks. We Bostonians have no cause to complain about New York traffic jams, but who needs a cause? And I actually found a metered parking space, which made me feel like a lottery winner.

After settling into the hotel room I called Thomas Thayer & Company, who had been Howard Holton's publisher from the very first book, and was informed that both Mr. Thayer and Fran Dixon, Holton's editor, were "in a meeting," and so couldn't respond to any questions I might have about whether or not Howard Holton had been working on a Boston-based true-crime book when he died.

"Is this a real meeting?" I asked. "Or are they just not taking any phone calls?"

"Both," the receptionist said, chuckling. "They're in a meeting and not to be disturbed unless it's a matter of life or death."

"Well, I'm dying, so ring me through."

"That won't work, Mr. Hawkins."

"I said I'm *dying*." I coughed and wheezed. Meg, undressing for the shower, shook her head—who was this lunatic she'd married?

The receptionist laughed again. "It has to be life or death for *them*, sir, not for you."

I left my name and number and hung up, defeated.

Dying wasn't good enough. What kind of publisher wouldn't take a call from a dying man? Answer: a smart one.

But how about a *dead* man? It was worth a try. I called again, got the same receptionist. Holding a plastic water glass near my mouth, to disguise the timber of my voice, I said, "Howard Holton to speak to Tom Thayer. This is an emergency."

"Hi again, Mr. Hawkins."

I dropped the cup. "How did you recognize my voice?"

"You sound like 'Cheers,' sir. You know, the Boston TV show?"

"What if I'd tried being Howard Holton the first time?"

"That might have worked, but not now. Bye-bye, sir, it's been a real hoot. And I'll be sure to tell Mr. Thayer you called."

I rolled into the steam from the shower, and said, "Guess what? I'm a real hoot."

Megan said she knew that already.

The Lion's Head is on Sheridan Square, in Greenwich Village. Steps going down from street level make it tough sledding for a wheelchair, but with Meg tipping me back for balance I made it with a minimum of fuss. And was again reminded why I rarely go into a place that is not easily accessible—not because of the difficulty, but because I loathe drawing attention in that way.

Oh the poor man on wheels, and the poor girl with him, is she a nurse?

That kind of attention.

No complaints about the Lion's Head clientele, though. I found myself being regarded with, at most, mild interest. The next thing I noticed was that the walls were papered with bookcovers. All kinds of books, from thrillers to belles-lettres. Almost immediately you sensed that this was a smoky, unpretentious neighborhood hangout that attracted writers and journalists and working-class stiffs who wanted an honest drink and a chance to trade lies with patrons who didn't think that literature had to start with a capital *L*.

No wonder it had been Howard Holton's favorite locale. In addition to his bookcovers, there was a glossy, signed publicity photo of the full-bearded author wearing outdoorsy garb and holding up a large fish. Why not? He'd been called, with good reason, the Hemingway of crime.

A big, bald-headed bartender was punching combinations on the jukebox as we entered.

"I'm takin' requests," he said. "Limited requests. No rock, no schlock. Coltrane or Miles?"

"The Train first," I said. "Then bring on the brass."

That was how we made friends with Tommy the bartender.

"Sure I knew Howard H. Holton," he said. "Howard Henry Holton. We called him H-Man. You a pal of his?"

"I've read his stuff," I said.

We had a late lunch at the bar—tortellini with red sauce—and cultivated Tommy between other customers. He was more than willing to talk about H-Man, who had been, we soon gathered, popular with just about everyone who frequented the Lion's Head.

"We had a little memorial service for him last fall," Tommy said, planting his beefy elbows on the mahogany bar. "Place was jammed. Pete Hamill was here, wrote a piece about it for the *News*."

"So I guess there's no truth to the rumor that Holton was a mean drunk?"

Tommy shrugged. "I've seen him drunk. Never mean. Not in this bar, and not at home, either."

"At the Sturne Royal?" I said.

Tommy laughed. "The penthouse? Are you kidding? That wasn't home for H-Man. I'm talking about his place on that island."

"Nantucket?"

"Sure, Nantucket. The little cottage he bought out there with his own dough. Money he earned from his books, he was real proud of that, not a penny from his wife's family. Every year a bunch of us would go up there, fish for blues and stripers. Mostly blues."

Meg gave me a look. This was pay dirt, and we had to sift it carefully. "My mom lives on Nantucket," she said, casually. "We got married out there."

There are times when the best thing to do is sit back and shut up and let Megan handle it. She has a way of getting strangers to confide in her, and not only female strangers. Pretty soon Tommy's expression had softened and he was telling her about the last day in the life of Howard Holton.

Tommy had been there, sitting in a rocker on the screened-in porch when H-Man caught his last fish.

"You been out there, you know how those big combers can come in on the south side of the island? Rolling all the way from Spain, or maybe Africa? They kind of hump up when they hit the beach and all of a sudden this big mother comes crashing down— *wham*—when you least expect it."

He used his hands to shape the waves, a big burly man making a picture in the air.

"What happened, H-Man hooked into a big blue and he didn't want to let it go. He's jogging along the beach, giving it line, and then the fish starts to run. Maybe it felt the wave coming in, I don't know. So H-Man is holding the rod high, like you're supposed to, and he runs into the water, up to his hips. He's screaming at the damn bluefish and we're all watching from the porch. Watching H-Man, see, because he was hav-ing such a good time with the freakin' killer fish. When, like I say, all of a sudden *wham*, a wave breaks right over him."

Tommy paused, buffed the scarred bar with his forearm, studied the shine.

"He doesn't come up. We see that, right away we break from the porch, run into the surf. Five of us, okay? And we dove and dove—you can't see nothing in the water, it's all foamed up with the surf and the sand, and we found the rod but we never found H-Man. The rip tide got him, is what happened. But you know the weird thing? Like I say, we found the rod and we reeled in the line and there was the bluefish, still on the hook. Like it was waiting for H-Man to finish the job."

Seeing that we had finished the tortellini, he brought us coffee without asking. Meg sipped, pro-nounced it good, and asked if there was anything strange about the way Holton had died.

Tommy gave her a squint. "Other than that a fish killed him? No. I guess his number was up."

"So you have no doubt that he really drowned?"

He shook his head.

"'Course I'd love it if he didn't," he added with a small, secretive smile.

8

For some reason returning to the city of my birth always brings a local nursery rhyme to mind. The kind recited to a child being bounced on your knees: *Here we go to Boston, here we go to Lynn, look out little boy or you're going to fall . . . in!*

The idea was to open your knees and catch the kid just before he tumbled to the floor. It was not, despite the description, a form of child abuse. Kids loved the *you're going to fall . . . in!* part.

Besides, rare is the Bostonian who can't be improved by a bump on the head.

All the way north I kept thinking about Howard Henry Holton. H-Man to his friends. Did he know he was going to fall in? What evidence did Tasha have that Holton was alive, other than a similarity in the style of a novel written by an admitted fan of her late husband?

We were back at our Beacon Street digs by noon—Meg returned to Standish House for an afternoon of work almost immediately. Fiona's book was just one of twenty or so she was responsible for in any given year.

"Thank God for small blessings," she said, munching an apple on her way out the door. "Harold Standish has gone sailing in the Bahamas for the next ten days. So if you could just fix this little problem before he gets back?"

"There are lawyers involved," I reminded her. "Don't get your hopes up."

"Think about it this way," she said. "If Harold Stan-

dish fires me, you'll be so mad you'll tear up your contract and then you'll have to find another publisher for
the Detective Casey series. And that will make you so
anxious you won't be able to write any more Casey
books—which means you'll have a lot of trouble getting another publisher."

"So I need to 'fix this little problem' to avoid writer's
block? Is that how you see it?"

She kissed me. "Think of helping Fiona as helping
yourself."

The lady called a few minutes later.

"Meg?"

"On her way to the sweat shop, Fiona. Can I take a
message?"

I could sense her hesitation. She didn't entirely
trust me.

"Someone is watching me," she said finally. "I
know that sounds crazy."

"What kind of someone?" I asked.

"A man. He's sitting out there in his car right now.
And I'm almost sure the same man followed me back
from your place the other night."

"Has he threatened you?"

"He just watches me."

"Describe the vehicle," I said. "Plate number, if possible. And then tell me exactly where he's located."

That's how I happened to be back behind the
wheel almost before the seat had a chance to cool.
Fiona had rented a small loft in the Fort Point Channel
area, on the way to Southie. Cross the bridge, take the
second right off Summer Street, she'd said, then right
again. It was an area of brick warehouses and trucking
firms and, lately, a small colony of artists who had fled
the rapacious real estate market on the other side of

the channel. No doubt it would soon become chic and then suffer the familiar rape by speculators, but that hadn't happened yet. The streets were still rutted and barren, and it remained, for now, a cold, industrial quadrant boxed in by railroad tracks. Not a place you would call a neighborhood, unless you had a diesel engine for a heart.

There was nothing remarkable about the late-model sedan Fiona had described. The neutral color blended into the background of grimy snow and cinderblock. It did, however, have tinted windows that made it hard to see the man slumped behind the wheel.

I pulled up close enough to block his door and rolled down my window. The guy inside didn't respond. I tapped the horn. Now he looked up at me and shrugged.

I tapped the horn again.

He rolled his window down a few inches.

"Find another place to park, pal," he said.

I said, "Excuse me, have you ever seen one of these?" and showed him the gun I'd brought along. "Beretta 70S. Nice handling pistol, very accurate at close range. Keep your hands where I can see them," I added.

"You're making a mistake," he said, but kept his hands on the wheel.

"Happens all the time," I said.

He still hadn't looked directly at me. I could make out a putty-colored face, a bulbous nose, and sandy hair protruding from under the brim of a snap-visor cap.

"I've got the plate number," I said. "All I have to do is look it up. Want to tell me who you're working for?"

"You know I don't," he said.

"So you might be casing that loft across the street. Planning a robbery. Lot of break-ins in this area."

"Do me a favor?" he said. "Point the peashooter somewhere else? It might go off."

"Yeah," I said. "It might. Accidents happen."

"What do you want?"

"Nothing personal," I said. "This can't be the first time you've been burned. Just tell me who ordered the surveillance."

"You know I can't do that."

I threatened, cajoled, promised to have a kid sugar his gas tank and slash the tires if he didn't speak the truth. He didn't budge and he never turned to look me in the eye, although it must have been tempting with a .38 pointed at his head. He had no way of knowing there was no bullet in the chamber, but he did know that direct eye contact would make it easier for me to identify him later. He was a pro. So he kept his hands on the wheel and stared straight ahead.

"Well," I said. "This has been fun. You're going to sit out here in a cold car, you ought to invest in a pair of mittens. I'll bet you've got hemorrhoids, too."

"Doesn't everybody?" he said.

I couldn't help it, I kind of liked the guy. I pulled away, circled around the freight tracks and back, and then parked in the space he had vacated.

Fiona was waiting for me in the street. She'd seen the whole thing from the loft.

"So who was he?" she said as I followed her into the warehouse. "What does he want?"

"Operative for one of the larger security outfits," I said. "That's my best guess. We can run the plate number, see if it clicks with any of the licensed firms."

"But what does he *want?*" Fiona's voice broke and I noticed the wet spots on her cheeks. Her hair looked matted and unkempt, as if she hadn't had the energy to groom herself after a bad night.

The freight elevator was an open cage, and noisy. I loathe open elevators and kept my eyes closed until it shuddered to a stop.

The loft smelled of new paint, and was sparsely furnished. There was a small railway kitchen with a simple table and one chair. The bedroom was wherever she unrolled her futon. Most of the place was a work area that overlooked the looming presence of South Station, located directly across the channel.

"I like to watch the trains," Fiona said. "I find it very soothing."

Her desk was a sheet of plywood on sawhorses. She had a word processor, boxes of diskettes, a letter-quality printer with the tractor feed linked to a box of fanfold paper. Reference books were stacked on the bare plywood: a dictionary, *Bartlett's Quotations*, the Katz film encyclopedia, the *Chicago Manual of Style*. A partial manuscript was divided into chapters, each in a separate file folder. It all looked very neat and professional.

"Your next book?" I asked, lifting a file folder.

Fiona took the file. "Please," she said. "Not an early draft. It's a superstition of mine."

I sighed. "Fiona? You're in big trouble. Tasha Sturne Holton is not inclined to drop this, believe me. Her husband's body was never recovered and she seems to think he might still be alive."

"But that's ridiculous. A dozen people saw him drown."

I shrugged. "I don't think this is about *Sea Change*, or who really wrote it. This is Tasha's way of smoking out her husband, if he's still alive."

"He's not," Fiona said. "I'm sure of it."

"How can you be so sure?"

She hesitated, turned away from me. "Because he would contact me. We were . . . friends."

"Lovers?" I said.

She shook her head. "Never that. We had a similar, ah, problem." Fiona stood at the window, staring out at a bleak March sky that was the color of dirty ice. "Alcohol dependency," she said in a clenched voice. "We were both bad-news boozers who wanted to kick and we went through it together. Climbed back out of hell. That can bring you closer to a person than mere sex, believe me."

"I do," I said. "That part of it, anyway."

It made sense. Fiona had the fragile toughness of someone who'd emerged from addiction and was now taking it one day at a time. She gave the impression of having a finely honed self-awareness, the certain knowledge that she would never be completely beyond temptation, that a return to her addiction was never more than a drink away.

"Let me see if I understand this," I said. "You and Howard Holton were hospitalized together?"

"Not exactly," she said. "We saw the same psychiatrist, for counseling. And we went to meetings together. Do you know anything about the A.A. program?"

"A little," I said. "Mostly what I've read in Larry Block's novels."

"Well, I was Howard's sponsor. I'd only been sober myself about six months, so it was really premature at that stage—to take on the responsibility of helping another addict. But he wanted me to and so I did."

"Before this you'd met him at The Raven's Nest?"

She turned from the window. "We had a few drinks after the book signing, talked about writing, the writer's life. How miserable he was, the lie he was living. Tasha."

"What lie was this, Fiona?"

She smiled tightly. "Tough guy, two-fisted novelist, woman chaser. He called it his 'bottle life.' This personality that took over when he was drinking, a part of himself that he didn't like very much. That he loathed."

"You said 'Tasha,'" I reminded her.

Fiona sat at her desk, bringing herself to my level. I could see the folds of loose flesh at her neck, the pallor she'd failed to cover with powder. I was aware, suddenly, of the effort she had to take each day in making a new face to show to the world. Fiona was skating on the thinnest of ice. She had to keep moving or risk falling through the mirror, back into whatever she'd been before she divorced herself from alcohol. I admired her nerve. The question of who was the real author of *Sea Change* was becoming less important to me—I wanted to know who Fiona Darling was, and how she had gotten there.

She said, "He seemed to think his life was phony. That he was failing Tasha. He kept saying that she needed a strong man in the family, and that he just wasn't up to it."

"A strong man?"

"Howard was on the Sturne board of directors, you know. A proxy vote Tasha gave him when they were first married—to make them more 'equal.' He didn't have any money of his own, not then. He was expected to take an interest in Sturne International, vote on important issues that came before the board. When the truth was he could have cared less."

"And things were supposed to get better if he quit drinking?"

"I think they *did* get better," Fiona said. "My impression was, Howard was more at peace with himself."

One of the side effects of writing crime stories for a living is that you're always looking for motive. And sometimes for the motive behind the motive. All the quirks and kinks and yearnings of the human heart, that is the only real mystery worthy of our attention.

Howard Holton had made a big change—but why then, and why in Boston?

"So," I said. "Was he planning to leave Tasha when he got himself straightened out?"

Fiona hesitated. "It wouldn't have surprised me," she said. "I got the impression their marriage hadn't really been a marriage, not for years."

"So you knew about his affairs?"

She shrugged. "I don't think they were all that serious. Not from what he told me. Chasing after women was part of his 'bottle life.'"

The bottle life. A persona Howard Holton had invented to keep the demons at bay. One Howard Holton had been the novelist, a brilliant and wicked pathologist of crime and high society. Another had been husband to Tasha Sturne, keeping an eye on the family business. Another had been the boon companion of Tommy the bartender. Still another had been the troubled mentor of Fiona Darling.

How many faces could a man present to the world before the bottle shattered? Before he gave himself up to the unexpected wave, the undertow of despair that must have been tugging at him all his life?

"You're stuck in the middle of this," I said to Fiona. "Fair or not. You're going to need a lawyer."

Fiona shook her head. "They'll crush me," she said.

"That's why you need a lawyer," I said. "Fitzy can recommend a firm that specializes in copyright law."

"Maybe I'll just give up," she said, running her hands over the slick, blank sides of the file folders. "I'll stop writing."

"That's crazy."

"Is it? What's so great about the writing life, Jack? Does it make you happy?"

I opened my mouth to say that, of course, it did and discovered the answer dying in my throat. Happy?

Did writing make me happy? Did writing make *anyone* happy?"

"Happy is a separate issue," I said, after giving it some thought. "Some writers are happy, some aren't. Okay, most aren't. Blissed-out types don't feel the need. But happy or miserable or demented or desperate or just plain boring, writers *write*, that's what they do, that's how they make sense of the world. As you well know."

"I thought I did," Fiona said. "Now I'm not so sure."

9

When Megan insisted that we install a cellular phone in the van, I'd thought it an absurd waste of money. Drive and call at the same time? It was dangerous, if not wasteful, and reeked of yuppiedom. Which just shows you how wrong stubbornness can make me. The van phone has turned out to be just another means of access to the world, making it that much easier for me to live an almost normal life. No more stopping to find a pay phone—a real project when you have to get a wheelchair in and out of a motor vehicle, even one that's especially equipped for that purpose.

I called Russ White from the red light at South Station, on my way back into the city.

"Crime desk."

"Are you buying or selling?" I said.

"That you, Jack? Who's dead?"

"Nobody's dead, Russ. Wait a minute, there *is* somebody dead, but it happened months ago."

Russ chuckled. "What can you do for me?" he said.

"I think you're a little mixed up," I said. "The question is 'What can I do for you?'"

"That's what I said, Jack. Think about it."

"So," I said. "If you've got time for word games, I guess you've got time to see me, huh?"

"I'll break out the champagne," he promised.

When I was a tyke there were four major dailies fighting for circulation in the city. Two remain, the fat-cat *Globe,* which dominates the market, and the scruffy, understaffed tabloid now known as the *Boston Standard.* The *Globe* has great sports coverage, the Spot Light investigative team, several readable columnists, and "Calvin and Hobbes."

The *Standard* has Russ White, possibly the best crime reporter north of Miami—in the same class as Edna Buchanan. Like Edna, Russ has an eye for detail that gives murder a human face and he never, ever, glamorizes violence, or those who live by it.

When I rolled into his cubicle, one of fifty or so in the rat maze of editorial offices, he was decanting a bottle of discount seltzer.

"I heard you and Meg got legal, that calls for bubbly," he said, handing me a plastic cup of fizz water.

"On Christmas Eve," I said. "This is old news."

"Until now it was only a rumor," he said pointedly.

"Ah," I said. "You want to know why you weren't invited. It was, as the saying goes, a small family ceremony. Me, Megan, her mother, and a Justice of the Peace."

"I figured Tim Sullivan for best man."

"Sully wasn't invited."

Russ looked surprised. "Not even Fitzy and Lois?"

"Not even."

He nodded, satisfied. Russ is a slender man with a thin, elongated face, active brown eyes, a pockmarked complexion, and a jutting bottom lip. His thick, rusty hair is going white in streaks and he tries to dress dapper, if only to irritate his publisher, who thinks that journalists should remain rumpled, turn in their copy on time, and shut up about unions, not necessarily in that order.

"So who died," he asked, "months ago?"

I told him about Howard Holton and how the Sturne family was getting ready to pounce on poor Fiona Darling. "They've already sicced a shamus on her," I said, "I've got his plate number."

Russ showed his teeth. "And you want access to my data base. Hence the visit."

"Hence," I said, toasting him with the plastic cup.

In the old days you had to know somebody at Motor Vehicles, and the going rate for pulling a plate number was ten bucks. Now you subscribe to a data base. It took Russ less than four minutes to determine that the car was registered in the name of Theodore P. Margolis, residing in Winthrop (pronounced Wintrup by the natives), just across the harbor from Boston. Russ immediately plugged Margolis into another data base, tugged at his lower lip as we waited, and then said, "Licensed through Fitzroy Security. The big boys. Surveillance rate is currently two hundred per hour per operative, electronics extra."

"Believe me," I said. "The Sturnes can afford it."

"You're sure it's her?"

"My best guess," I said. "Or her law firm. They probably throw an investigator at any potential lawsuit. Billing the client, of course."

"Of course. So they think Howard Holton is alive and well and living in the arms of his mistress? Any chance of that being true?"

"Slim," I said. "You want to leave your fabulously wealthy wife, it's a hell of a lot easier to file for divorce than it is to stage a drowning in the Nantucket surf. Why bother?"

"Still," Russ said, making a steeple of his fingers, "No corpse makes it interesting. Has he been declared legally deceased?"

"I thought it took seven years."

Russ shook his head. "Not always. And certainly not for a powerful family like the Sturnes. They might not be able to collect on an insurance policy until more time has elapsed, but for legal purposes—say the proxy vote on the board of directors—I'm pretty sure they could push for an early declaration."

"Except that Tasha prefers to believe that he's still alive. Or that's what her brother says."

Russ nodded thoughtfully. "Hey," he said, "how about this? Maybe she knows something you don't."

"The thought has occurred to me," I admitted. "Couple of things that might be helpful. Background on Fiona Darling. And any odd little snippets that never made it into the papers when Holton drowned."

"Odd little snippets," Russ said. "Sounds like a character in an Evelyn Waugh novel. So you think there's a story in this, and that's why I should do you this favor?"

"How about out of the goodness of your heart?"

"Come on," he said.

"What was I thinking?"

10

You think of me as a bit of a frump, conservative on a personal level. Right? Be honest. Would you ever guess I was an Elvis Costello fan? But think about it. How could a crime writer *not* be a fan of a rocker who sings about "Watching the Detective" and brags that "Every Day I Write the Book"?

So imagine Elvis Costello theme music as my van glides into Winthrop. Not so much gliding, actually, as creeping in heavy traffic along Shore Drive. The Atlantic Ocean looking as flat and gray as a banker's suit—just a flash of white at the cuff where the surf ripples.

I had called Fitzroy Security and asked for Theodore Margolis. Not in, they said. Doing my impersonation of a furtive informant, I mumbled something about a hot tip on a case he was working.

Still not in.

The dirt on Fiona Darling, I promised.

"This regards a current investigation?"

"That's what I'm sayin'. He'd wanna know."

"Can you leave a number? I'll call Mr. Margolis at home and have him contact you."

"Ain't got a numbah, lady. I'll try 'em tamahrah."

Everybody lies to private investigators, why should I be an exception? And now I knew that Margolis could be found at home. Home being a small gray ranch-style on Ocean Avenue. You really could see the ocean from there, if you stood out in the street.

I parked in the driveway, blocking the generic sedan with the tinted windows. Made a show of exiting the van, taking my time on the E-Z-Lift, because this wasn't supposed to be a sneak attack.

The man himself appeared on his front steps. Wearing a ragged white fisherman's sweater, antique chinos, and bedroom slippers. He was shaking his head and grinning.

"You son of a bitch!"

I waved from the lift, bumped my chair into the layer of slush at the bottom of the driveway, where the drain was blocked.

"Hey Ted! How's it goin'!"

Margolis picked his way over the dry spots, being careful in his slippers. "Let me guess. You've got a friend at Motor Vehicles."

"Access to the data base, Ted. This is a high-tech world. Is Ted okay?"

"Fine," he said, giving his head a rueful shake. "My mother called me Theo. My ex-wife called me . . . never mind what she called me. What, you figure I'll invite you inside, confess my sins?"

"I'd love a cup of coffee," I said. "We're maybe four miles from downtown Boston as the crow flies, it took me an hour. The tunnel."

"Yeah, the freakin' tunnel, I hate it."

He shouted the last part as a jet came in low over the beach, heading for Logan Airport.

"Ted, I'm sorry about the gun," I said. "It wasn't loaded."

"I had a guy come after me with a baseball bat once," he said, touching his bulbous nose. "Wacked me pretty good. I'm pretty sure it was a Yaz autograph model."

"Ouch."

"I never been shot at, though. Look, you come all this way, you're proud of yourself for making me, so come on in, we'll have coffee. But Hawkins? And, yeah, I know who you are—plate numbers really *are* a cinch these days—forget it about who's the client. You know I can't tell you that."

"Fair enough."

"So," he said, pulling up his garage door. "You write books, huh?"

I liked the way he directed me into his house the easy way, without making a fuss about the front steps. I rolled into the kitchen—remarkably neat and tidy for a middle-aged divorced male—and asked for a towel to dry off my wheels.

Margolis tossed me a dish rag without comment.

"Caf or decaf?" he asked, pointing at a drip coffee maker.

"Your choice."

"Oh hell," he said, "let's live dangerously. Little caffeine high can't be worse than having a .38 pointed at my ear."

"Ted? No bullet in the chamber. Honest."

"Yeah, and the check is in the mail. Look, forget about it. I didn't figure you for a shooter. Then when I looked you up—a kid at the office has read all your books—I figure this has to be an improvement on the usual enraged husband wants to knock my block off because I snapped him duckin' into a no-tell with a lady wasn't his wife."

"That happens a lot?"

Margolis bent his head down, showed me a long scar under his graying, sandy hair.

"That was a fifth of Jim Beam. Happened to be full, so the alcohol kept the wound clean. That's what the doc told me anyhow. Maybe he was just tryin' to cheer me up. I get depressed whenever somebody hits me."

Margolis had a dry, self-deprecating wit that made you like him. The same manner made him dangerous as an interrogator. You wanted to give him an answer, just to keep the conversation going.

"So," he said. "You're recently married and already you're sneaking a little on the side. And with your wife's client, too."

"Fiona? Come on. And she's an author, not a client. There's a difference, believe me."

"Yeah? She called you, right? J. D. Hawkins to the rescue."

"She's a friend."

He grinned, poured coffee into ceramic mugs.

"That's what they all say."

I decided to change the subject. "Most of the Fitzroy Security operatives are ex-cops. You, too?"

He chuckled. "Operatives? You been reading too much Dashiell Hammett. Work for private security firm, you're an investigator. Just like for an insurance company. And no, I was never on the cops. Navy Intelligence. I retired after twenty. Been with Fitzroy for almost ten now, they treat me good."

"The IBM of detective agencies."

"They hate that word: detective. Intelligence gathering, that's what we do."

"So now that you've been burned, they'll put someone else on Fiona Darling?"

"Fiona who? All you're getting out of me is coffee, Hawkins."

"I'll bet you were a tough son of a bitch in the Navy, huh?"

"I was a sweet guy," he said.

"Captain Margolis, USN. You *did* make captain?"

"I did," he admitted.

"Okay, Cap. There's been a mistake. A very wealthy family has decided to make life difficult for Ms. Darling. A big Fifth Avenue law firm is playing it heavy and now they've hired a big detective agency, security firm, whatever you want to call it, to put the screws to her. Really scare the hell out of her and, not so incidentally, her publisher."

Margolis was shaking his head.

"What?" I said. "I'm being paranoid?"

"I'm not saying your lady friend is the target. But if she was, we don't screw with targets. All we do, keep a log. Which a lawyer may have use for in a court case, or maybe not."

"Target" was an interesting choice of words, but I didn't mention it. I was in the man's house, drinking the man's coffee. That called for good manners. No insults, no sticking gum under the seats.

"She hasn't done anything," I said. "Her crime, she happened to be a fan of the late Howard Holton. But I guess you know about Holton, right?"

A shrug. "I've heard of him. What makes you think he's late?"

"He's been declared dead," I said.

"He has like hell."

"What?"

Margolis grinned. "It's not that easy. In the Navy we'd have said he was missing presumed dead. In the Commonwealth of Massachusetts they see it different. There's a whole legal process to get through. And it hasn't been got through, not yet."

"And you're part of the process?"

Another grin. He wasn't going to say. On the other hand he hadn't denied it.

"I've got a theory that Tasha Sturne Holton thinks her husband may still be alive," I said. "Do you?"

When Margolis shrugged a crease appeared above the broken nose.

"You seem like a decent guy, Hawkins. I'm gonna give you something here, so try not to throw it back in my face. Your friend with the fancy loft? Ask her who her landlord is. Who she pays the rent to—or if she pays."

"That's it?"

"That's a lot," he said. "Now if you'll excuse me, I

was about to take a nap. Old retired codger like me needs his beauty sleep."

A real gentleman, he held the door.

The answering machine cut in just as I rolled into the apartment, in a hurry for the ringing phone. I picked up and said, "This is the real me."

"Fran Dixon, Thomas Thayer Books. I'm returning your call."

I reminded Fran that we'd met several years before at a Bouchercon in Baltimore. A Bouchercon being a convention of mystery writers and their fans named in honor of Anthony Boucher, the critic and novelist.

"Howard Holton," I said. "The late and the great. You were his editor?"

"Guilty," she said. "What's the crime?"

"None that I know of," I said. "Will there be any posthumous publications?"

"Just one," she said. "The novel he turned in the week before he died. We're bringing it out on our spring list. Pub date in June, I believe."

"Any chance of getting a galley copy?" I asked. "I'd be willing to pay for it, of course."

Fran was silent for a moment. "What's this about?" she asked.

"There's a rumor that he isn't dead," I said.

"You mean like Elvis? Sighted at the Seven-Eleven?"

"Something like that," I said, wondering how Fiona would react if her book was compared to an Elvis sighting.

Fran was chuckling. "Is this a prank, Jack?"

"You don't think it's possible?"

"If he walks in my office I'll think it's possible."

"Howard told Brant and Tasha that he was making trips to Boston to work on a true crime book."

"News to me."

"He wasn't working on a true crime book?"

"Oh I suppose he *could* have been, for another publisher. But why keep it a secret from us? And it would be rather difficult to keep a true crime project secret—he'd be attending the trial, deposing witnesses and so forth."

"So you think the true crime stuff was just an excuse to visit a mistress?"

There was a long pause. Thinking it over before responding.

"*Cherchez la femme* if you like. I'm not going to comment. Howard's death hit us hard here. We liked him, we liked his books, we respected his privacy. I really can't say anything more than that."

"Fair enough," I said. "Will you send me the bound galleys?"

Fran got cagey.

"What are you expecting to find. A clue?"

"A clue would be nice," I said.

egan brought home Chinese takeout from a new place on Boylston called Totally Hot.

I pointed to my mouth and made gasping noises until she handed me a beer.

"I *told* you to pick out the hot pepper pods."

I blinked the tears from my eyes and managed to croak an acknowledgment of her superior wisdom. The cold beer helped, but my esophagus felt as if it had been invaded by a platoon of little men with flame throwers.

"This was stir-fried by the general who invaded Tienanmen Square," I said. "Bet you anything."

"I'm not ready to joke about Tienanmen Square."

"Megan, that was *years* ago."

"Slaughtering kids never gets funny, Jack."

"Well, can I joke about Howard Holton? He's dead, too."

"Joke away," Meg said, rolling her eyes.

"What," I said, "what if Fiona is fibbing?"

"Not funny."

"Irony can be funny, too. How ironic if Holton is still alive and he's using Fiona to front his novels."

"That goes beyond not funny."

"What if, for instance, our sweet Ms. Darling was living rent-free in a loft owned by Howard Holton?"

Megan dropped her dumpling in the red sauce.

"There might be an explanation," she said. It sounded lame and she knew it. "Is this on the level, Jack? Holton owned the loft?"

I described my visit to Theodore Margolis.

"They don't like the word 'detective,'" I said. "Conjures up the image of a boozy guy in a trench coat. Or a cop. Fitzroy Security likes to think of it as 'intelligence gathering.'"

"And this guy *told* you Holton owns the loft?"

"Dropped a hint. Russ White checked it out for me. All those data bases in the *Standard* computer system? He's having a hard time finding anything on Fiona—not even a birth certificate, so far—but he did confirm that Holton bought the loft last year, a month before he died."

Megan sighed. "There's more, isn't there?"

I nodded. "Someone has been paying the mortgage for the late Mr. Holton. In his name."

Meg closed her eyes. "I still don't believe it," she said. "I *know* Fiona wrote that book. I *know* it."

I knew what she meant because despite mounting evidence to the contrary, I still felt the same way. Fiona had made me a believer, too. Could she be such a skilled con artist that she'd known exactly what buttons to push on an editor *and* a novelist—not to mention a bookstore owner who knew her share of author types?

"Maybe there *is* a way," I said. "Fiona Darling is a writer, we both agree. But maybe she didn't write *Sea Change*. Maybe she got it published as a favor to Howard Holton. Maybe the book she's working on now really *is* her own."

Megan was shaking her head. "Jack, we discussed revisions in *Sea Change*, okay? Some minor problems I had with certain characters and scenes. In some cases she made changes, in others she convinced me the material needed to stand as it is, with flaws intact. 'Keeping the rough edge,' she calls it. Jack, let me tell you again, *I know she wrote the book.*"

"Let's call her," I said. "Let's get together with Fiona

and make her tell us what she's hiding. It's your career, too, Meg. You've got a right to know."

I was rolling toward the phone when it rang.

"J. D. Hawkins?"

The voice was oddly familiar.

"Yes," I admitted. "Who is this?"

"Brant Sturne." He giggled. "Bet you never expected to hear from me, huh?"

"Well, this *is* a surprise, Brant," I said, signaling to Megan. "What can I do for you?"

"For me? Oh, isn't that sweet. Well, let me see," he said playfully. "You could send that beautiful wife of yours over, have her rub my back."

"Brant," I said. Meg, listening in, made a face.

"Just kidding," Brant said. "Well, not *really* kidding, but who am I kidding, right? I'm here, Mr. Hawkins. Right here."

"Where's here, Brant?"

"Bah-bah-Boston. Beantown. The Hub of the Universe! I'm up here on, oh I can't decide, is this business or pleasure? Both, I hope."

"Brant," I said. "Could you be a little more—"

"Specific?" he said, cutting me off. "That's what Tasha always says. But specific is so *boring*. Specific is, well, *specific*, you know? The way I do it, things just happen."

"What things, Brant?"

He had a fit of giggles, so high-pitched and sustained that it made me wonder if he'd been sniffing nitrous oxide. No, I decided, laughing gas was way too tame for the likes of Brant Allan Sturne. He'd be into some drug designed especially for the penthouse set. The kind of drug that had a monogrammed capsule and was ingested only at the best parties.

When the giggle fit had subsided he said, "Mr. Hawkins, have you ever seen a ghost?"

"Only in the movies," I said. "Cary Grant in *Topper.*"

"This could be more fun than some old movie," he said. "If you'd like to meet Howie's ghost, come on over."

"Where are you, Brant?"

"At the hotel."

"The Sturne Royal?"

"What do you think, silly? That I'd stay at the Ritz?"

"We'll be right there," I promised. "Is Howard with you now?"

"Ghost Howie? No, but he'll be right along. He promised, and Howie *never* broke a promise to me. Not ever."

In the bad old days, Park Square was an outpost on the edge of the Combat Zone. The Trailways Bus Terminal siphoned off a steady stream of the bent and twisted, with lockers sometimes used for drug deals, and the upstairs restrooms famous for bartered sex. Those with actual cash to trade could find cheap booze and twangy entertainment at the nearby Hill Billy Ranch, a favorite with the bus station cowboys. And if steam and sweat and strong hands was your pleasure, the Turkish Baths were just around the corner, as were, a few blocks away, the Naked Eye, the Kit Kat Klub, and any number of beer-drenched dives that promised coed topless dancers. My friend Fitzy used to remark that the "coeds" were enrolled at "Pasties College on the G-String Bill"—and Fitzy would have known.

That's all gone now, bulldozed into a bottomless pit that has lately emerged as the "new" Park Square. Showpiece of the square, overlooking the Public Garden, is the Sturne Royal Boston. Also known as the "golden tower," on account of the metallic facade, and to wiseguys as the "golden shower," because of the hosing the developer took while the tower was under construction. A city commissioner and a gang of building inspectors were convicted, eventually, of soliciting bribes, and the developer had gone into receivership, but the Sturne Royal had finally opened, several years behind schedule. Despite the construction and real estate scandals, it was emerging as Boston's premier luxury hotel.

The Sturne Royal had one major problem, as we quickly ascertained. No parking.

"Are you joking?" I said, leaning out the window into a flurry of fat, wet snowflakes. "You *must* have parking."

The doorman stood dry under an awning, reciting from memory. "Our apologies, sir. The facility is not available at this time. There are several nearby parking facilities—the front desk will validate your ticket for a discount—or you can leave the vehicle here with our valet service."

"And where do *they* park it?"

"Wherever they can, sir."

It took us roughly twenty minutes to find a garage on Stuart Street and work our way back to the hotel, Megan on foot and me pushing through the slush.

"I guess it's fine for the limo crowd," Megan said, brushing snow from her eyelashes. "You know, visiting executives, tourists who arrive by air, and so on."

"I think the phrase you're looking for is 'screw the local traffic.'"

"Now you mention it."

"It strikes me that the parking place we finally got is approximately as far from the hotel as our apartment is."

"We should have left the van and hoofed it," Megan said.

"But, snowy night in March, naturally we drive."

"Naturally."

The snow was turning to rain as we arrived at the lobby. The doorman managed to look through us—dumb schleps, we should have taken advantage of the valet service. They were, however, wheelchair accessible at the main entrance, which is more than you can say for the Ritz-Carlton.

Brant wasn't quite as well known at the hotel as we'd expected.

"Brant Sturne? Do you have a room number?"

"I assume the top. He's used to heights."

The desk clerk fetched her boss, the floor manager.

"Brant Allan Sturne," I told him. He looked blank, polite but blank. "Heir to the family fortune? The Sturne in Sturne Royal? Ring any bells?"

He got it, finally. "Oh, *that* Mr. Sturne? I assume he's in the family suite? Let me check?"

He picked up the phone, pasted a hotel smile on his face, and fluttered his eyelids. "No one answers?" he said. "Sorry? Is there something else I could do for you?"

"Where's the family suite?" I asked. "We'll check it out. He's expecting us."

"So sorry, sir? If you'd care to leave a message? We'll see it gets to Mr. Sturne? And then perhaps he can instruct us regarding your visit?"

I said, "You've been a big help?" and backed away from the desk. Experience tells me not to expect much from those who make every statement a question. Also Megan was starting to blush and it was best to withdraw gracefully before she gave the floor manager the tongue-lashing he deserved—being chased out into the slushy night by security guards was not my idea of a good time.

"Any bright ideas, Mr. Question Mark?" Meg said as we edged away from the reception area.

"I'm thinking."

"I could pull a fire alarm," she offered. "See if Brant runs out in his bare feet. Count the toes going by."

"You're not serious."

"Males are bound to go extinct, like the dinosaurs. They have such tiny little brains."

"Go ahead," I said. "Take it out on me."

The lobby was crowded with couples parading in glad rags, heading for various swanky Sturne Royal restaurants and lounges. Mingling into the throng at the elevators was no problem. Megan's theory was that the "family suite" would be on the top floor, facing the Public Garden. "You know, home away from home," she said. "And I'll bet you a nickel Brant has the drapes closed. This is an inward boy, Jack."

"With tongue in cheek?"

"Don't be disgusting."

We ambled around the top floor and found nothing that resembled a "family suite." Finally we resorted to that time-honored technique so often employed in the best hotels: bribery. Forget the chambermaids— they're underpaid and afraid of losing their jobs, and/or their green cards. Go directly for the bellhops, the kind whose hands are stained dirty green from all the bills they palm.

Our man was Nick, according to his nametag, a spry, crinkly-faced gentleman in his late sixties. "Yes, sir, I know Mr. Sturne. That is, I brought up his dinner. You want to see him, though, he has to make the request, then I'll be glad to escort you. Sir and lady both."

I explained our difficulty with the front desk, the small matter of Mr. Sturne not answering his phone.

"I could, of course, knock on the door, determine if

he's receiving. Have to be later though," he said craft-
ily. "I'm pretty busy just now."

"How busy?" I said, opening my wallet.

We settled on twenty dollars as fair compensation.
Nick removed keys from his pocket, led us through a
locked door marked STAFF ONLY, and into a buffed marble corridor of condominum suites. It was like going
through the looking glass—a whole wing of the hotel
we hadn't realized existed.

"This is the best of the best," he said, ticking over
the floor on his bandy legs, as if prepared to break into
a dance routine. His heels didn't really have metal
taps—that was my imagination. "Some of these places
sold for two million," he added with evident pride. "And
I don't mean pesos."

The door to the Sturne suite was unlocked, part-
way open.

"Maybe the young gentleman stepped out," the
bellhop said.

There was something about that open door I didn't
like. Maybe it was the shadow that seemed to flicker
from inside, or the whirl of lights reflected from a crys-
tal chandelier. I pushed forward and the bellhop had to
step back or risk having his little shoes run over.

"Hold on, sir. You can't go in there."

"Follow me," I said, pushing faster. "Make sure I
don't steal the towels."

The inside foyer was a small echo of the grand
New York penthouse. I didn't have time to admire the
tall vases this time, or the fresh white orchids. The
door to Brant's bedroom was open and I could see
him dancing under the chandelier. Tick-tock, a human
pendulum.

His toes just brushed the top of the unmade bed.

It was the bellhop who screamed, not Megan. I
want to make that very clear. Meg is not a screamer,

she's a doer, and what she tried to do first was lift Brant out of the velvet noose that was looped to the chandelier.

There was a lot of dead weight there, but she grabbed his knees and heaved. He slipped free and came thumping down on the enormous bed in a jumble of arms and legs, the black silk robe caught up around his waist. Megan scrambled out from under the body and began the ritual of administering CPR. Attempting to clear his air passages, thump his heart, and so forth.

I wanted to tell her to stop, Brant Allan Sturne was just as dead as dead could be, but when Megan Drew gets it in mind to save a life, she can't be dissuaded.

She was right about the drapes though. They were closed.

s it happened, Lieutenant Detective Timothy Sullivan had the flu, so the case was caught by Sergeant Detective Larry Sheehan. He was glad to see us, looking jaunty in a surprisingly clean trench coat. The new London Fog didn't disguise the tough little guy with the duck's ass haircut and the permanent squint, the Sheehan we all knew and—well, maybe loved isn't the right word.

"Hey, Jack! Hey, Megan! Hey, whaddaya know, I come over to check a guy hung himself, who do I find? Familiar faces."

The way Sheehan talks it was more like *fam-ail-yuh fade-sez,* but then a New York receptionist had accused me of sounding like a refugee from "Cheers," so who am I to criticize? Suffice it to say that Detective Sheehan uses the Chelsea vernacular—you want to sound like him, gargle with battery acid, then stuff pebbles in both cheeks and sneer with just your bottom lip.

The jovial, glad-hand attitude was mostly for show, or to get a rise out of me. Lately we've been operating under a truce of mutual respect, but for years Sheehan hated my guts. I was the guy who got his pal Brad Dorsey thrown off the cops for stopping an all-in-fun bullet with my spine. I was the guy who sued the department and won. And worse, I was the guy who'd used a thinly disguised version of homicide detective Larry Sheehan in several books—as a lowly sidekick, yet.

We had, as the saying goes, a past.

"So," Sheehan said, looking from the chandelier to

the corpse splayed on the bed. "You been hanging out with the deceased, or what?"

Megan spit. "You mind if I rinse my mouth out?" she asked. There were tears in her eyes.

"Go ahead," he said. "But not here. I understand you gave him mouth-to mouth?"

Meg nodded.

"Nice," he said. "Use a bathroom down the hall. This one is secured, a couple hours anyhow."

Meg ducked out the door as the EMS crew maneuvered a gurney into the room. Two uniformed men were going through the motions, taking pictures, unreeling tape measures. The Homicide Unit routinely investigates all "unnatural" deaths, even obvious suicides, but as yet no Crime Scene Unit had been dispatched—they would await Detective Sheehan's decision before proceeding with a full investigation.

"I think it was an accident," I said.

"Guy dangles himself from the shandy, it's an accident?" Sheehan said with a grin. This was a good one, he wanted to hear more.

I told him we'd visited the deceased in New York, and that Megan had noticed a collection of erotica that indicated an interest in hanging as a form of sexual arousal.

"Oh yeah?" Sheehan said with interest. "I heard of that. So you're saying this guy didn't mean to kill himself? He was getting his rocks off?"

"I'm saying it's a possibility."

Sheehan got a cagey look as he tapped a Lucky Strike from a pack he always carried in his shirt pocket.

"The deceased—Brant Sturne—does that mean what I think it means, the family who owns the hotel?"

"Many hotels," I said.

"So this is VIP shit, I better be nice?"

"I didn't say that," I said.

"I said it," Sheehan said, puffing energetically on his cigarette. "Talking to myself, see, for what you call my own edification." He jerked his thumb at the dead boy on the bed. "This is big money, indentured shysters, the whole enchilada. I gotta be sharp."

"You mean being rich makes a difference?"

Sheehan snorted smoke, grinning with just his eyes.

"Gimme a break," he said. "You know it does."

Meg and I had not discussed what we would say to the detective, but neither of us saw fit to mention Fiona Darling. It wasn't, at that point, a matter of withholding evidence. Fiona was not directly involved— Brant had called out of the blue, tantalizing me with the ghost of Howard Holton—and there was no reason to drag Fiona into it yet.

Not as we saw it. And we held nothing back about Brant or his habits or the doubts about Howard Holton's death.

"You telling me he said 'ghost'? Come on, what is this?" Sheehan's brow was furrowed into V's and the characteristic squint made his eyes look shut.

"My impression, he didn't really mean ghost," I said. "He meant Holton was alive and coming to see him. And that we could see him, too, if we hurried."

"And did you," Sheehan said, "hurry?"

"We had trouble finding a place to park. Trouble getting up here—he wasn't answering his phone."

"Yeah, no kidding."

A medical examiner had signed for Brant's body, which was bagged and removed. The detective wasn't sure about an autopsy—would the family object?—but an autopsy could be ordered with or without permission under the circumstances of probable suicide.

"I'm estimating almost forty minutes elapsed," I said. "You agree with that, Meg?"

"I wasn't looking at my watch, but that sounds right."

"And this 'ghost,'" Sheehan said, taking notes, "is a dead mystery writer, like you?"

"Thanks, Larry."

"Hey, I meant he was a writer like you, only he was dead. Now is that a fact?"

"Holton vanished in the surf," I said. "No body was recovered. Brant seemed to think he was still alive."

Sheehan sniffed, tapping an unfiltered cigarette against the back of his hand. Already he was working on the third, chain-smoking his way through another homicide. Or accidental death, if he cared to see it my way.

"Okay, we got the deceased calls you, says hurry over, and while he's waiting he decides to play with himself. Kinky shenanigans with the velvet noose, only he slips and—oops!—it really happens. That the way you see it?"

"Like I said. It's a possibility."

"Another possibility," Sheehan said. "The guy *intends* to hang himself, he wants you to find him. The old last-phone-call scenario. You'd be surprised how many check into a nice hotel, they intend to knock themselves off. Like they don't want to make a mess at home."

"He didn't sound suicidal," I insisted. "He sounded . . . excited."

Another full-body shrug from Detective Sheehan. "From what you say, he was into hanging as some kind of twist, right? So maybe he was excited about the idea of killing himself."

"Larry, I just don't know," I said. "All I'm thinking, if there's any possibility it was accidental, give him—his family—the benefit of the doubt."

"I dunno, Jack. Brother of mine, would I rather everybody think it a clean suicide, or was he some kind of pervert killed himself in a sick accident? Get my point? I don't really see the benefit here, the accidental death angle."

"Maybe you're right," I said.

"Tell you what," he said. "I'll push for an autopsy, maybe the ME can tell." He glanced at Meg, cleared his throat. "You know, if he was, um, aroused at the time."

Meg was just standing there, staring at the empty bed. She'd come back with her eyes red and wasn't really paying a lot of attention to Sheehan, or to me for that matter.

"Media is gonna love this," Sheehan said. "Spoiled rich kid, the velvet noose."

"They won't know about the kinky angle unless you tell them," I said.

"Come on," he said. "This is a big hotel. Everybody works here knows all the dirt by now. You think they won't talk? You think your pal Russ White won't get the goodies?"

He had a point. It was the kind of sad and furtive end that would rate page 3 in *The Boston Globe,* but might make a front-page splash in *The Standard.* "Noose of Death," that sort of thing.

"Tell you what," Sheehan said. "I'll play it tight. No comment until after the post. In deference to the family."

"That's the smart way."

"And just to cover my ass, all this money died in here, I'm going to call for the Crime Scene Unit, let 'em do their thing. I'll need prints to match from you and Megan."

"I'm sure you've got our fingerprints on file."

"Yeah, but it would be easier, believe me, we get fresh. Do you mind?"

We left Detective Sheehan interviewing hotel staff.

First in line was bellhop Nick, who had shown us to the door. He looked a little gray around the gills now, not the least inclined to bust a new dance step.

In the elevator Megan expressed her anger.

"How could he do a thing like that?" she said. "How *could* he?"

"You're mad because you couldn't save him."

"Sheehan may go for the accident baloney, Jack. I don't."

"Hey, it's okay to be angry. A suicide is a terrible waste of life."

Meg gave me a look as the doors slid open. "Suicide? I'm not mad at poor Brant. I'm mad at the ghost."

"Holton?"

"He did it," she said vehemently. "I don't know how he managed it, or even if he was really here, alive, but somehow he's the reason that boy is dead."

Outside, the slush had turned to snow, covering the bare trees in the Public Garden, and any of the homeless who hadn't managed to find shelter for the night. In Boston, as elsewhere, the inns are always full.

13

You know what's going to happen if we go straight home?"

Meg shook her head. She was in the seat beside me, hunched up inside her parka, not making eye contact. After the outburst about Holton, she'd lapsed into silence, nodding when I talked but making no comment.

"Russ White will run us down. Remember, I already put him on to the Sturne family, doing us a favor. Naturally he'll think I owe him the gory details of any story that emerges. Meg? Are you listening?"

She nodded, staring at the dim whiteness of Stuart Street.

"I think we should go see Fiona. Right now."

That brought her out of it. She looked at me and said, "Fine, let's do it."

The streets were relatively quiet, in what was developing into a heavy snowfall. We crossed the Fort Point Channel without incident and parked near the warehouse.

Howard Holton's warehouse.

"The lights are on," Meg said, getting out of the van.

I rolled to the back, lowered myself to street level on the E-Z-Lift. Looking up, I saw snow falling, white and soap-flake soft, through the glow from the loft windows. There were, I ascertained, no familiar sedans in the area, no sign of any Fitzroy Security investigators.

"Find a way," I urged Megan as we headed for the door to the warehouse.

"Huh?"

"To make her talk. If Holton really *is* alive, Fiona knows."

"I'll do what I can, Jack," Meg promised.

The door that led to the freight elevator was locked. I pushed the buzzer, assumed it rang in the loft. We waited. No response.

"I'm sure she's there," Meg said, stepping back to look up at the lights.

I rang again.

"Maybe the bell is busted. I'll keep trying, you go to the van, call her on the cellular phone."

Meg came back five minutes later to report that there was no answer.

"You thinking what I'm thinking?"

"We have to get in there, Jack."

A break-and-enter turned out to be no big deal. One of the truck-sized bay doors was unlocked—an oversight that screamed "Burgle me!" in this part of the city. Megan lifted it, heaving against the counter-balance springs, and we scooted into the dark interior. Various smells: crankcase oil, damp steel, the dank, mousey pong of a warehouse.

"You hear any claws skittering, let me know."

"This place had an attack dog, he'd be chewing us by now," I said.

"I was thinking rats."

"Think of them as squirrels," I said, "with slender tails."

The echo made her laugh sound hollow and forced. As my eyes adjusted to the dark I saw a semi-trailer, machine parts stacked in pallets, the dim rectangle of an open door.

"That's the freight elevator ahead."

Ah, Megan Drew's eyesight. Several years of poring over manuscripts hadn't weakened her night vision. I called her "Bat Woman" once but she took exception. It was my contention that bats would be flattered by the comparison. Meg insisted that wasn't the point, she didn't want herself likened to a small air-borne rodent, thank you very much.

"Fiona?"

"You heard something?" I said.

"Ssssh." Then, "No, I guess not."

As a mode of transportation, I'm not wild about freight elevators. They should elevate freight, that goes without saying. Human cargo, well, some of us humans prefer not to see the naked elevator shaft or all the moving gizmos, any of which might fail at any moment.

"We could go up one at a time," Meg suggested. "If you're worried about the weight."

"It's rated for a full ton. I checked the permit last time."

"So you'd rather we went up together?"

"Stop being nice just because I'm nervous."

"Fine, Jack, get in the damn elevator."

We got in. Meg hit the button and the machinery delivered a catalogue of groans and shrieks as the cable began to wind, drawing upward in a series of shivers and shudders, not all of them mine.

"You know what to do if it falls?" I said. "Jump up just before it hits bottom."

"What'll *you* do."

"Save yourself," I said. "And I heard that smirk."

"Can't hear smirks, Jack."

"I have a keen ear."

I shouted Fiona's name as the freight elevator creaked to a stop at loft level. No reply. Not a creature was stirring—and Ms. Darling had not impressed me as a sound-sleeping type.

Meg lifted the safety bar, stepped into the loft. "Fiona?"

"Nobody home," I said. "Would she leave the lights on?"

The loft was one big room, with the exception of the bath and a few closets. Not a lot of hiding places— and Meg checked them all. The futon hadn't been unrolled. There was a spaghetti pot in the sink, awaiting transfer to the dishwasher, various implements on the counter, as if Fiona had been in the act of preparing a meal when she stepped out for a few minutes.

"Look at her desk," I said.

If you haven't copped to it already, take it from one who knows: Megan Drew is quick on the draw. She glanced at the desk and swore.

"How could she?"

The desk was bare. No word processor, no floppy disc files, no manuscript.

"Check the medicine cabinet," I suggested.

"Why there?"

"You're a woman. What does a woman grab on the way out if she leaves in haste and isn't planning to come back any time soon?"

I had no idea what a woman would consider essential but I was pretty sure Meg would know.

She came out of the bathroom slowly, shaking her head.

"If I had to guess, I'd say she scooped everything into her purse. Like she was in a hurry."

"And forgot to shut off the lights."

"I know this looks bad," Meg said, planting herself on Fiona's work chair, staring unhappily at the empty table. "Maybe she had a reason."

"Sure she had a reason."

"Jack, there *is* such a thing as coincidence."

If Megan had been trying to make me laugh, it worked. We both know about coincidence. In fiction coincidence can be a plot accelerant, even a means of diverting a reader's attention from the real culprit. But the reality of Brant's sudden death and Fiona's sudden departure was about as coincidental as Jerry Ford's pardon of Richard Nixon.

"Could be that the landlord tipped her off," I said.

"What?"

"Howard goddamn Holton. He was supposed to meet Brant at the hotel, right? Maybe he had something to do with making Brant dance from the chandelier and maybe he didn't—but work from the premise that one way or another he knows the boy is dead."

"And he calls Fiona?"

"A theory."

"You think Fiona ran off with him?"

"If he's alive. If he's not, then she's got another accomplice, someone we don't know about."

"Another theory?"

"Free associating. Off the top of my head."

Meg stood up from the desk, folded her arms.

"I hate mysteries," she said.

14

It was a bad night for dreams. Meg got up several times, trying to be quiet about it, and camped in the living room.

"Try hot chocolate," I called out. "I'm counting sheep, we can compare notes."

Meg slunk back into the bedroom, nuzzled up from behind.

"Sorry."

"Don't be. You're waiting for the phone to ring, right?"

I could feel her chin move as she nodded.

"You figure she owes you a phone call."

Meg sighed. "That's what I figure. This is more than editor-author, Jack. Fiona is my friend."

"There's one problem here, from her point of view."

"What's that?"

"I might pick up the phone."

Meg was quiet, thinking it over. "She doesn't trust you?"

"Maybe it's a gender thing," I said. "I got the impression Fiona doesn't trust men, period."

"She told me she liked you."

I turned, snapped on a light. "What else could she say?"

"I just—I don't think you're part of this, Jack. I don't know *what* to think. Not about Howard Holton or Brant Sturne, or why Fiona ran away. I just don't *know*."

There's a theory that equates weeping with weakness. A theory disproved by Megan Drew, who is anything but weak, but who sometimes weeps in moments of anger, frustration, or joy.

So what we did was lie awake together and wait for a call that never came.

Russ White had the courtesy to refrain from calling until the sun had risen, although it remained almost invisible under a thick March sky. A kind of luminous source that made the Cambridge skyline into a set of jagged, gray flannel teeth.

"Thank you, thank you, thank you."

"Russ?" I said, holding the phone away from my ear.

"This could be the best thing that's happened since Charles Stuart jumped to a conclusion off the Tobin Bridge," he said, sounding hyper. "You see our page one?"

"Haven't had the pleasure."

"Death by Velvet, Heir Swings From Chandelier.'"

"Russ, please. I haven't had my breakfast."

Megan was up, wrapped in a robe, her feet bare. She made a face, shook her head. Meg likes Russ personally but hates the *Standard*.

"This has the feel, Jack, of a big one. A never-ending story. And I'm a little hurt you didn't call."

"Why should I call?"

"With gory details. You and your lovely wife discovered the body. You saw him swinging, Jack. I could have used you. Instead we went with the bellhop, first person account: 'I brought him dinner, then he dangled.'"

"Russ, ease up. We knew the boy. We sort of liked him."

He ignored me. This was news, the best kind for a crime reporter. Big money, kinky death, with a promise of more secrets to be revealed in the next edition. This was his business, his blood, and Russ was understandably intoxicated with the prospects.

"Ms. Darling isn't answering her phone," he said. "I thought possibly she was a house guest."

"Not here," I said.

"You wouldn't fib to me, not after I hooked you into our data base."

"I might, but she's still not here."

"Have it your way. So what did Mr. Velvet have to say before he hung himself. *If* he hung himself."

Meg was pouring coffee for both of us and glaring at the phone. She has the bizarre idea that everyone, even journalists, should respect the dead. And this despite being married to a guy who makes his living thinking up ways to kill off fictional characters.

"Brant said he was in town, asked us to stop by. We did. He was dead when we got there. And what do you mean *if?*"

"*If* is always the best part, Jack. You know that as well as I do. There's the *if* that says he could have been involved in an erotic act, the near-death climax routine. And you should have heard Sheehan skipping around *that* theory, trying to say it without saying it."

"I can imagine."

"The other *if* is almost better. What if somebody put him up there on the chandelier? Got any likely candidates?"

Megan, with ears cocked, shook her head.

"No," I said. "Look, Russ, it's been nice chatting."

"The kiss-off," he said. "So, will I see you there?"

"Where?"

"The postmortem. A little gurney bird told me the results might be interesting."

Lieutenant Detective Tim Sullivan was back on the job, despite a lingering flu bug. His mild blue eyes were obscured by a mist on his glasses, and he kept polishing the lenses with a crisp white hankie, to no avail. Every time he cupped his nose to contain a sneeze, the mist reappeared.

"You look like hell," I said.

"I *feel* like hell."

"You're sick, that's why you're letting Sheehan brief the press."

He shook his head. "Larry caught the homicide. It's his. He's witnessing the autopsy so he gets to brief the press."

Sully and I go way back. At a time when no cop on the force could utter my name without gritting his teeth, Tim Sullivan treated me like a fellow human being. And when I needed a witness, a detective who would testify that the vice cop who accidentally shot me was unbalanced, a known wacko, Sully took the oath and told the truth.

There are those who think that the dapper homicide detective in my Casey novels is based on Tim Sullivan. I can only say that Casey drinks schnapps and Sully doesn't drink period. Casey is married to the feisty Naomi, whereas Sully is a career bachelor. They do share a weakness for mail-order chess, an acerbic wit, and an air of diffidence that some find off-putting.

The difference is, I made up Casey and Tim Sullivan is real. Real enough that he claims never to have read the books.

· We were in an underheated room at the police morgue, awaiting release of the ME's preliminary brief, usually delivered by an attending homicide detective directly following the autopsy. Not an officially announced press conference, but those beat journalists who knew the ropes were in attendance. All print reporters so far, the video freaks had yet to arrive.

"Larry keeps it? No matter how big it gets?"

"Now, why should it get bigger?" Sully said, blinking rapidly. He had a sneeze coming on. "You expecting a rash of apparent suicides?"

"You read his report?"

He nodded. "Yeah, yeah. The deceased called you, mentioned a man who drowned in Nantucket. What have you got for me, Jack, a limerick?"

"I'm starting to think Howard Holton might still be alive. Brant apparently thought so, and Tasha hired Fitzroy Security to check it out."

"Tasha? Oh right, the sister. And Holton was her ex-husband?"

"They were still married when he disappeared in the surf. I gather it wasn't a perfect marriage, but nobody mentioned anything about a divorce."

"My mistake. Sheehan said you knew this guy Holton."

"Not exactly. I never met the man."

Sully frowned.

"But I may have given Larry that impression," I amended. "Holton was a crime writer, we knew a lot of the same people. And I *do* know his books."

Maybe it was the virus that made Sully sarcastic.

"That will be a big help I'm sure," he said. "Unless you're saying that the victim stood on a stack of Holton's novels to get his head in the noose."

"Come on."

"And by the way, we need to talk to this other woman, Fiona Darling."

"What's Fiona got to do with this?"

"Where is she, Jack?"

He was bearing down now, very serious.

"I can read the papers," he said. "Your pal on the *Standard* played her large. Helpless victim of lawsuit threatened by powerful family."

Past experience had taught me that withholding information from Detective Tim Sullivan was like pulling the pin on a grenade that's stuck deep in your pocket. So I told him about our trip to Fiona's loft. He was interested enough to stop polishing his glasses.

"She was gone, what, an hour after you discovered the body? Appeared to have left in haste?"

"Maybe there's no connection," I said. "A coincidence."

He put his glasses on, shoved them up with his
forefinger, a characteristic gesture he shares with my
fictional Detective Casey.

"And pigs have wings," he said. "She was made,
Jack."

"What?"

"At the Sturne Royal. Seen in the vicinity of the victim's suite. One of the chambermaids remembered
a lady, her description fits your friend Fiona Darling to
a T."

A door opened and Larry Sheehan entered, a cigarette in the corner of his mouth. Appearing almost
amiable for those who didn't know better. His off-
the-record look. He spoke briefly to the forensic pathologist's assistant who had accompanied him out of
the morgue, then sidled over to where Tim Sullivan
was standing.

"Should I read the whole thing, you think?"

"Your call," Sully said, studying his nails.

Sheehan glanced at me, smirked.

"This is playing just like you promised."

He gestured at the reporters, who were doing a
crabwise dance, shuffling to follow Detective Sheehan
while still keeping their collective eyes on the door to
the morgue, as if expecting or hoping that the ME, no-
toriously loose-tongued, might himself appear.

"I think I'll avoid details," Sheehan said. "Just give
'em the gist."

Sullivan's approving nod was almost impercepti-
ble. Larry marched back to the center of the room and
the crowd followed him, leaving Sully and me more or
less to ourselves.

"What," I said to him. "Brant was poisoned? Shot? What does everybody know that I don't?"

Sully gave me a look. Was I playing dumb? He decided I wasn't.

"Postmortem confirms what the ME surmised last night," he said. "Brant Allan Sturne was strangled. Compression of the vagus nerve, resulting in near instant death. The velvet noose, the chandelier, it was all for show."

"Murder," I said.

Sully choked back a sneeze. The television crews, I noticed, were just starting to arrive.

"Was there ever any doubt?" he said.

15

R uss White bought me a late breakfast at a Washington Street cafeteria. A place so franchise-perfect that it almost made me nostalgic for the mystery-meat specials at the old grease-stained Waldorf's. Almost but not quite.

"I can't be bribed," I said. "Not even with crenshaw melon and sweet rolls."

In the old days Russ would have been rushing back to make deadline for an afternoon edition. But when the McGary chain took over, the afternoon and evening editions were dropped and now any story he developed using the new strangler angle would not hit the streets until the following morning, long after television saturation. That meant he needed some trenchant, tabloid-sizzling detail that was liable to be overlooked on the local news.

He had time, in other words, to develop his sources. Or bribe them.

"Luncheon at the Ritz," I said. "Of course you'll have to wear a tie. We can fuss over those little watercress sandwiches and I'll drop some revolting tidbit about Brant Sturne."

"Watercress? Don't do me any favors."

"All I'm saying, Russ, everything I know, you know. So what'll we discuss here, the Red Sox?"

"Not unless there's a crime involved."

"Russ? Every season is a crime against nature, the Red Sox. You hear the one about Bill Buckner? He wanted to come back to Boston but he missed the plane—it went right between his legs."

Russ grimaced. It was an old and tired joke.

"You want to change the subject, fine," he said. "Out of the kindness of my heart I ask you to this perfectly adequate place, and you start mewling about how it's not the Ritz Café and imply I'm trying to squeeze a, quote, revolting tidbit, unquote."

After the outburst he sighed, studied the Formica environment, succeeded in looking vaguely wounded.

"I guess you were up late, too," I said.

"Haven't been to bed yet. Am I overreacting?"

"A little, maybe."

He hesitated.

"Thing is, I *did* have a question or two regarding Fiona."

"No idea where she is," I said. "Cross my heart."

Russ shook his head. "Not that. More like where she's been. I told you I keep coming up blank? I was thinking maybe Fiona Darling is a pen name, that's why I can't pull it on any files."

"I'll ask Megan, but I don't think so. She goes by Fiona, I know that much."

"Reason I ask, I've been trying to pair them. Howard and Fiona. So far all I've confirmed is the loft—he owned it, she lives there, or did. Rent free, apparently, unless she paid in cash. I've got another reporter on it now, checking out the business angle. Looking for a money-type motive."

I said, "Holton was known to be generous. Maybe he was helping out an unknown writer."

Trying to convince myself, really. Russ, although sympathetic, wasn't buying the premise, not without evidence.

"She and Holton kicked the booze together, right?"

"That's what she told me," I said.

"Because I located the joint where he kicked and they have no record of Fiona Darling. Fresh Start, this place in the South End."

"They *gave* you that information?"

"No, of course not. Their data base—insurance payments and so on. It's pricey, two grand a week, total of eight for the whole treatment."

"Wow."

"Hey, the business of sweating out alkies has come a long way since Dropkick Murphy's."

"Fiona could never afford that. Eight thousand dollars was more than her advance for *Sea Change.*"

"Right. Which is why I thought her good and generous friend Howard Holton might have picked up the tab."

I concentrated, tried to dredge up the memory of my last—most recent—conversation with Fiona. I could see her in winter light at the window, speaking in a clenched voice, telling me that she and Howard Holton had shared the experience of emerging from a booze-tinged hell.

"As I recall, she didn't claim they were actually hospitalized together, but I'm pretty sure they shared a psychiatrist. Does Fresh Start have an out-patient clinic?"

Russ said, "I can find out."

Alcoholism is no joke, especially to a novelist. The casualty list is extensive, from Hemingway to Capote. There's something about inventing lives on paper that leads to the cold, compelling fusion of a perfect martini.

Writer-drinker temptations may have made the nearly abstemious Megan Drew all the more attractive to me. Drink to excess with Meg and you'd soon find yourself drinking alone. For that reason and others, my present intake is occasional if not always moderate.

There was a time though, before I was reborn on

wheels, when alcohol was an important part of my life. A beer or two at lunch to shorten those long gray afternoons as a tech writer. And four or five well-paced bourbons at the Shield or the Plough or the Eliot Lounge; story-collecting bourbons, night-enhancing bourbons. Good honest whiskey, the kind you could smell on your own breath, the kind that tastes strong and clean in the shot glass. No cheating with untasted, fruit-diluted vodka, the secret elixir of the "problem" drinkers.

Brad Dorsey's all-in-fun bullet cut short my bourbon nights. Social drinking gets tough in a wheelchair—the doors are too narrow, the tables too close, the bar too high. And friendly drunks, when they're not looking away with booze-startled shame, want to pat you on the head.

I hate being patted on the head.

Still, I knew enough about alcohol abuse to fake an addiction, at least for the purposes of extracting information about Howard Holton. This was made easier by current standards of what constitutes a problem. No need to appear at the door with the screaming fantods of classic withdrawal—any level of abuse would do, especially at eight grand for the cure.

I called from the van, wobbled the handset to make myself sound a bit shaky, and was advised to present myself to a Fresh Start "evaluator," who would assess my condition.

"You know the South End?"

"I can manage," I said.

I was directed to a side street about six blocks from Fitzy's law office, very convenient if my old pal ever decided to kick the habit. The four-story building had the look of a converted rooming house. Not so long ago there were hundreds of these old brick dames in Boston, shelter for the down but not quite out, weekly or even daily fees financed by small Social Security or retirement checks. Then the upscale-condo-conversion mania swept through town in the guise of "gentrification," putting most of the old gents on park benches or subway grates.

Of course only a befuddled reactionary would see a connection between real estate inflated by yuppie investors and homelessness. In a free market you have the option to buy your own park bench. Right?

An entrance is important—I wanted to make a convincing impression. Staggering was out. I made up for it by slumping in my chair and staring into the middle distance as I rolled through the refurbished mahogany doors. This was method acting—calling up anguish isn't all that difficult for a paraplegic, we know where it lurks.

Maybe I overdid it because a staff member rushed to my side.

"Sir? Are you the gentleman who just phoned?"

I nodded miserably.

"I'm Muffin, your evaluator."

"Muffin?"

"I know it's silly. Blame my parents."

Muffin escorted me to a nicely furnished office suite—the parlor of the old rooming house, I guessed. It was in perfect South End taste: restrained modernity in a carefully restored interior. Paneled walls hung with city scenes by Childe Hassam, plaster ceilings with a lot of droll trimwork, triple-glazed security windows, lovely antique carpets, and a functioning fireplace.

My evaluator sat in a wingback chair, tending the fire. Walk in on the scene and you might have assumed I was applying for a job in one of the old Boston trading firms.

"Tea leaves from Ceylon," I said. "Egyptian cotton."

"Pardon me? Did you want some tea? Herbal or de-caf?"

"Excuse me. Nerves. I tend to babble." I held out a trembling hand, dropped my eyes, and muttered, "I'm so ashamed."

"Acknowledging dependency is nothing to be ashamed of, Mr., ah, Hawkins," she said, glancing at a form on her clipboard. "Could I have your insurance card, please?"

"I'll pay cash," I said. "That is, if you think you can do anything for me. Is cash okay?"

Muffin smiled. We both knew that cash was always welcome.

"I'll need a bank reference," she said.

I mentioned my bank, named an individual who worked there. Described the source of, and grossly in-flated, my annual income. Muffin dutifully filled out the form.

"I get it," I said. "You're a *financial* evaluator. I assumed you'd evaluate my drinking problem."

"We're getting to that." Muffin flashed a perfectly nice smile. "First things first."

Having established that I had the necessary bucks, we proceeded to the next questionnaire. My substance abuse.

"The old term was alcoholism," Muffin said. "We find that too restrictive. Many of our clients have de-pendency problems that don't fit the parameters of ac-tual physical addictions. That is, if they stop ingesting the drug—or the alcoholic substance—they don't nec-essarily go into withdrawal. At least not physical with-drawal."

"No pink elephants," I said. An addict trying to make light of his situation.

"Snakes are much more common. Also bugs. We had one gentleman who saw little blue men, but he was later diagnosed as schizophrenic. But as I said, our typical abuser manages to function at almost a "normal" level, holding down a job and so forth." She glanced down at her checklist. "Mr. Hawkins, how would you evaluate your level of dependency?"

I'd given some thought to this, wanted to sound reasonable, given my appearance—and the fact that I'd come in sober. "Four or five drinks every night," I said. "Except last night. I haven't had a drink in thirty-six hours."

A glance at my watch to show I was counting.

"Excellent start," Muffin said. "How would you describe that intake in ounces?"

"Pardon me?"

"You say 'four or five drinks.' Are these one-ounce drinks, two-ounce, a full glass?"

I shrugged. "Two ounces, I guess. Maybe more by the end of the night."

"And in the morning?"

"I feel like hell. Can't concentrate. That's why I want to stop."

"But you don't take a drink in the morning? How about a Bloody Mary?"

"Sounds delicious, can I have one?"

Muffin chuckled to show she appreciated my sense of humor.

"Seriously," I said. "I'm a whisky vampire. Only drink after the sun goes down."

"What made you want to stop?" she said.

I'd thought about that, too, and settled on a half-truth.

"I'm having trouble with my latest book," I said. "The words won't come."

"And you think this is related to your drinking?"

"Don't you?"

"If you think it is, it is." Muffin checked off a few

boxes on the form and looked up with clear, wheat-brown eyes. "And of course there's always the possibility that you ingest more alcohol than you care to admit."

"I'm admitting I have a problem. I'm considering paying you people a hell of a lot to help me stop. Why would I lie?"

"Because abusers lie, Mr. Hawkins. Almost without exception."

I tried looking miserable and ashamed: score one for the evaluator.

"We do have an opening," Muffin said. "We ask that all first-time clients commit to our four-week cycle. Of course one cycle may not be enough, depending on individual needs. The first forty-eight-hour period is in the detox ward. Once you've cleared detox, you'd have a private room and unlimited access to our counseling staff."

I put my head in my hands and sighed. "There's no other way?"

"Not if you're serious, Mr. Hawkins. Changing a dependent life-style takes a tremendous amount of effort. On your part *and* on our part."

"I heard you had a day clinic."

"Well . . . yes, we do. But a case like yours requires a total commitment. And our day counseling sessions are usually reserved for those who have already undergone the full detox and evaluation."

I fiddled with my brakes, showing nerves. The thing that disturbed me here, I was getting a kick out of lying to Muffin. Also it was a little disconcerting, how readily she saw me as a problem drinker, substance abuser, whatever.

"You people helped a friend of mine," I said. "Actually, *two* friends of mine. One of them kicked here, as an inpatient. The other went just to the clinic, apparently, but anyhow they had a psychiatrist in common."

Muffin made a face. This was a complication and she didn't like complications.

"Thing is, I'd like to see the same shrink."

"All of our consulting staff are qualified," she said. "Who did you say recommended us?"

"Howie," I said. "Howie Holton. And his girlfriend Fiona. They both got straight here."

You could tell the way Muffin squinted that at least one of the names was familiar.

"Howard H. Holton, the novelist," I said. "And Fiona Darling. She's a writer, too. Fiona told me their shrink was simply fabulous. That's who I want to see."

Muffin stood up, holding the clipboard in both hands like a salver.

"This is most unusual," she said.

"Please," I said. "I'm desperate."

Muffin gave me a look that said she agreed whole-heartedly. Then she excused herself and left me to tend the fire alone.

16

The shrink had the wide shoulders, thickened neck, and buoyant stride of an athlete.

"Dr. Foster," she said, shaking my hand. "Call me Helen."

If I'd had to hazard a guess at Helen Foster's line of work, tennis pro would have come to mind. And not the kind who gives lessons at your local club, either.

Dr. Foster folded herself into the wingback chair like a puma curling to spring. Tawny blond hair cut short, cool gray eyes, and more self-confidence than a lifeboat full of Dale Carnegie graduates.

"So," she said. "How's Howard?"

Lying to Muffin was one thing. Lying to Dr. Helen Foster would have been like toying with the Grand Inquisitor.

"Howard is dead," I said.

Dr. Foster nodded, never taking her eyes from me. We both knew he was dead and we both knew I wasn't strictly on the level.

"A tragedy," I said. "Swept away by the undertow. I heard you did marvelous things for him, though."

"Howard told you that?"

"Fiona did."

Dr. Foster knitted her fingers together, cupped them over her knees. She was wearing a smoky-blue cashmere skirt that showed a lot of nicely toned leg muscle. Later my friend Fitzy would remark that the good doctor had thighs that could crack coconuts. To get the image right, bear in mind that the effect was very attractive. For all her coiled strength, this was not a muscle-bound woman.

"Fiona?" she said.

"Fiona Darling. Howard's friend. She was his sponsor in AA."

The doctor shook her head firmly. "Don't know her."

"She was a patient of yours," I said. "A novelist, like Howard."

"I'm sure I'd remember, even if she *wasn't* a novelist, Mr. Hawkins. I have an excellent memory for clients."

"Maybe she was using a different name," I said. "You know how writers are."

Again the firm head shake. "Mr. Holton recommended no one to me. I'd remember that, too."

"Would he have been seeing anyone else? Another psychiatrist?"

She thought about that. "Possible but unlikely. He would have told me. Howard was a man of extreme intelligence, well aware that consulting two psychiatrists at the same time is counterproductive, if not dangerous."

"Dangerous?"

"To the psyche. To the chances of full recovery."

"From alcohol dependency."

"From anything, Mr. Hawkins, including substance abuse."

"So he never mentioned a lady friend who was a writer? Who he was helping with a book?"

"If he did I wouldn't tell you, or anyone," she said. "Is that what this is all about?"

"Excuse me?"

"This phony attempt to check into the facility," she said. "Is it because you're looking for information on Howard Holton?"

Exposure time. This is when smiles get brittle, when lies are burrs in the throat. When it becomes prudent to cough up a small bit of truth.

"Fiona's in trouble," I said. "I'm trying to help."

"Playing games with us isn't going to help anyone, Mr. Hawkins."

"Fine," I said. "Let's quit playing. You're right, I came here looking for information. Have you heard from Howard lately?"

All trace of amusement and tolerance melted away. "Mr. Holton is dead, how could I hear from him?"

"The body was never recovered. Maybe he faked his disappearance."

"That's a crazy idea."

I shrugged. "Hey, you're in the business of crazy ideas, right? All I can say, there are certain indications that Howard Holton may be alive. For instance, someone has been paying the mortgage he took out on a building here in Boston. And last night his brother-in-law claimed to have talked to him."

I got her there. The surprise widened her eyes, and chilled them, too.

"You mean Brant Sturne," the doctor said. "He killed himself. I heard it on the radio this morning."

"You knew Brant?"

Head shake. "Howard discussed his family relationships, naturally."

"Naturally," I said. "But Brant didn't kill himself. Somebody strangled him and tried to make it look like suicide."

Dr. Foster stood up, folded her arms, stared at me the way a skilled butcher looks at a side of beef. Deciding where to make the cuts, how much fat to trim.

"If you're a policeman, show me some ID."

I raised my hands in surrender. "I'm not a cop. Okay, I lied about a drinking problem, but that's it. I really am a friend of Fiona Darling and she really was a friend—possibly more than a friend—of Howard Holton. He must have mentioned her, she was an important part of his recovery."

Dr. Foster turned her back, grabbed the tongs, and poked at the dying fire. I could sense her thoughts ticking. She was buying time, thinking something through.

When she turned her face was an expressionless mask.

"Never heard of Fiona Darling," she said, "and as far as I know, Howard Holton is deceased. Now if you will excuse me."

"Doctor, please. If Howard Holton was prone to violence or homicidal fantasies, now is the time to say so. You can't claim professional privilege for a client who is supposed to be dead."

"You've got three minutes," she said. "After that I make a call, see if we can't have you arrested."

She stalked out, leaving the door open.

I was pivoting the chair, lining up with the file cabinets, when Muffin came back. She stood there with her hands on her hips and said, "Don't even think about it. Two minutes and counting."

I took my time.

Muffin followed at a discreet distance and then held the lobby door while I pushed through. As I paused to turn my collar up against the stiff March wind she said, "I had you right all along. You *are* an abuser."

"Not of booze."

"Of trust," she said.

egan came home early, wearing a Mona Lisa smile.

"You'll never guess," she said, shrugging off her parka.

"Fresh out," I said. "Give."

"Fiona called," she said airily. "Care for a cup of tea?"

I followed her into the kitchen. "This is cause for celebration?"

"I was worried about her."

"Where is she?" I said. "What did she say?"

Meg put water on to boil, spooned loose tea into a pot. "We didn't actually *talk*," she admitted. "Fiona said, and this is pretty close to a direct quote: 'I just wanted you to know that I'm okay but you won't be hearing from me again until this whole rotten mess blows over.'"

"That's it?"

"That's enough," Meg said, perching on a stool. She paused to kick off her boots, then hooked her stocking feet on a rung. "What more do you want?"

"It's not what *I* want. The cops are looking for her. She's wanted for questioning."

Meg was exasperated. "Jack, I thought maybe she was dead. I mean the possibility existed, okay? Now I know she's alive, I want to feel good about it."

"Fine. Do a few hand springs. Send up balloons. But that doesn't change the fact that Fiona was spotted at the hotel last night. In the vicinity of Brant's room. Did she mention that, in this one-way conversation?"

The kettle began to sigh, building up to a sizzle. Meg just stared at me, processing this latest information on the unreliable Ms. Darling.

"A positive ID?" she asked.

"Enough so Sully and Sheehan want to talk to her. I should say Sheehan—Larry's in charge of the case."

"Jack, you don't seriously believe that Fiona strangled a two-hundred-pound male and then strung him up from a chandelier?"

I shook my head. "That's not the point, Megan. The point is, she's been lying to us. That should be obvious by now."

The kettle began to whistle. I described my visit to the folks at Fresh Start as Meg poured boiling water into the pot, glanced at her watch, noted the time. She's as meticulous about brewing tea as she is about editing manuscripts, always striving for clarity and strength.

"No record of Fiona getting treatment?"

"No record of her *paying*," I said, "in the way of insurance vouchers. According to Russ White and his trusty computer. And I think Dr. Foster was telling the truth, at least about never treating Fiona Darling."

"But hiding something else?"

"I got that impression. Something she knew about Howard Holton. Not that it matters. Psychiatrists are like priests, they never share a confession."

When the tea was ready Meg poured.

"We got a postcard from Harold Standish today. 'Dear Girls, the sailing is simply terrif.'"

"Girls?"

"That's why we all love him, Jack. We girls think he's simply terrif. But it did remind me, he's due back late next week. He'll want to play publisher again and the lawsuit is still pending. There's been some discussion about recalling *Sea Change* from the distributors."

"Will that happen?"

Meg shook her head, prompting that familiar bounce of auburn hair that never fails to give me a pleasant shiver. "Doubtful. Closing-the-barn-door sort of thing. The fact is, the book is selling better than we expected. If it keeps shipping at this rate we might even order a second printing."

"Hard to believe," I said.

"I could show you the figures."

"No, no. Hard to believe that the publication of a novel caused all this. Legal threats, a murder, an author who goes on the lam."

Meg's smile was grim. "It *is* a crime novel."

"There has to be something else, Meg. The book was just the snowball that got the avalanche rolling. The more I think about it, the more I think it all started with Howard Holton drowning. Or not drowning."

Meg shrugged. "Why not go for it?"

"What?"

"Take a position. Assume that Holton really is dead and that his death wasn't accidental. Assume he *was* murdered. Find out who wanted Holton dead, work forward from there."

I was looking for clues in the bottom of my teacup when Tasha Sturne Holton called. Or rather her lawyer did, to summon us into her presence.

The Sturne Royal Boston. Tasha had not been installed in the family suite, for obvious reasons. That remained sealed with yellow crime-scene tape. We'd been directed to another unit on the same floor. The layout was identical to the suite where Brant had died, except this time the shades were not drawn across an expanse of glass that faced the frostbitten Public Garden. From this height you could see trees cased in ice, the duck pond clotted with a layer of snow that glowed darkly under the glare of the streetlights.

Tasha answered the door herself, wearing a black leotard top, tight black jeans, black heels. Mourning in America.

"Oh," she said, glancing first at me, then at Meg. "Oh."

Tears rolled from her open, unblinking eyes. "Thurston," she said in a hoarse, pleading voice, "Thurston, it's them."

Her attorney appeared, pushing a bar trolley. He had his jacket off, sleeves rolled up, showing off the kind of well-muscled forearms that result from excessive raquetball with influential clients.

Tasha fled inside, bumping a slender hip against the trolley. Thurston Breen sighed wearily, came forward to shake hands.

"Good of you to come," he said. "These are the times, eh?"

"Pardon me?"

"That try men's souls," he said. "Tasha is in shock. Naturally. We shuttled up here this morning. I'm not sure why, exactly—the arrangements could have been handled from there—but Tasha felt she had to come. Had to *see* it."

Tasha called from the next room, "I hate flying. Everyone shoved together inside a big tin can? It feels like dying. But I had to come. Brant all alone in a strange place? I had to." She leaned around the corner, dabbing her eyes. "I'm okay now. It was just, seeing you both, I remembered."

What she remembered, she told us over drinks poured by the lawyer, was that Brant had told her we were fun.

"That means he liked you. Brant only liked fun things, fun people."

I glanced at Meg. This was new. I'd never thought of myself as a fun person. "You know we talked with him in New York?"

"He told me, yes. Thought it was a great joke, hiding you in his room. And then that policeman, the one with the awful haircut, he said Brant called you just before he died. That you two discovered the, um, that you found Brant."

Bad haircut meant Larry Sheehan, who was still doing his best to keep Brylcreme in business.

"Meg tried to revive him," I said. "We were too late."

Thurston Breen, Jr., glided back into the room, having donned his suit jacket. Driver, bartender, it made me wonder what other services he performed for his client.

"Damned decent of you," he said, leveling weary blue eyes at Meg.

"Yes," Tasha added. "I don't know if I would have had the . . . courage."

"I've had CPR training," Meg said, coloring with embarrassment. "It's reflex. I'm just sorry we were too late."

Tasha shuddered, gulped at her drink.

"I have to know," she said. "Please tell me. Why did Brant call you? What did he say?"

Thurston, sitting with his legs crossed, waited impassively. He had the look of a man who had spent the night comforting a distraught woman and was now emotionally depleted.

"Your brother was cracking jokes," I said. "Being very light and witty. Said he couldn't decide if he was in town for business or pleasure. Said he hoped it was both."

"What business?"

I shrugged. "When I asked him if he could be more specific he laughed it off."

"Laughed?" Tasha said in a small, childlike voice.

"Yes. He said you were always asking him to be specific. He was amused by the idea." I didn't add that the fit of laughter had been so prolonged it made me wonder if he was high on something other than life.

"Brant mentioned me?"

I nodded. "And then he asked me if I'd ever seen a ghost."

"He what?"

"Your husband's ghost," I said. "He seemed to be . . . kidding. Making another joke. I asked if Howard was there in his room and Brant said no, but that he'd be right along because he had promised and Howard never broke a promise."

Tasha buried her face in her hands. Her thin shoulders began to quake and the trembling resonated throughout her body. Thurston stood up and patted her on the back. I've seen saloonkeepers polish the bar with more passion—that neutral touch convinced me that whatever Tasha and her attorney shared, it wasn't physical intimacy.

The trembling never quite stopped but after a little while Tasha settled, took a deep shuddering breath. "Brant always loved Howard," she said. "They had a special bond."

"Your brother told us that you think your husband is still alive."

She nodded miserably. "It's a feeling I have."

"Just a feeling?" I said.

"He was a careful man, Mr. Hawkins. And a very strong swimmer."

"Strong swimmers sometimes drown," I reminded her. "Inhale a pint of water and you can lose consciousness almost instantly, no matter how strong you are."

Tasha made a dismissive gesture—she'd heard all

this ease-of-drowning nonsense before and wasn't buying. "Brant had the same feeling. We went out to the island, to that little cottage Howard bought, and we walked the beach. I expected to feel him there, you know? Some vibration of his death. But there was nothing. No feeling at all. He was just . . . gone."

I was about to comment when Megan's glance told me to shut up, that this wasn't the time for any sardonic one-liners about psychic phenomena.

"Not like here," Tasha said, glancing at the wall to her right, in the direction of the family suite. "I can feel Brant all around me. He died badly."

She covered her face again. This time her attorney didn't intervene. Comforting the bereaved wasn't in his contract, or possibly he was aware of how lamely he handled it—or maybe he was just bored by the prospect.

Meg, sensing a need, accompanied Tasha into the female privacy of the bathroom. In a few moments the muted sound of weeping carried into the room.

Thurston got up, poured us each another drink. "It's this sibling thing," he said. "Very powerful bond."

He made it sound like a rare blood disease.

"Having a brother murdered is a traumatic experience," I said. "She's doing pretty well, considering."

"I suppose," he said. "Listen, you mentioned Brant said he was up here on business. He happen to say what business, exactly?"

"If he did, I'd have said so."

"Of course."

"What business *might* he have had?" I said.

"Oh, family stuff," Thurston said. "You know."

"'Fraid I don't."

"Hotel things," he said. "The new facility here has had its problems."

"So?" I said. "Brant was interested in hotel management? I thought he just clipped his coupons and slept late."

Thurston laughed. "Oh, someone else clipped the coupons for him, you can be sure of that. You're quite right, Brant wasn't involved in the day-to-day management of the company. But he is, *was* a Sturne, and he *does* have voting proxy for a rather large block of shares. I thought possibly he'd been recruited by one of the board members—political infighting, that kind of thing."

I tried to imagine Brant Sturne involved in political infighting and failed. Unless, of course, they had allowed him to attend board meetings in his black silk jammies.

"You're looking for a motive," I said. "A reason why he needed to be killed."

Thurston was uneasy. "I suppose I am. But to tell you the truth, I can't really imagine Brant being so *involved* in anything."

"Tell me," I said. "Do *you* think Howard Holton is alive?"

"Tasha seems to think so."

"But do you?"

The disbelief showed on his face. "Oh, I suppose it's theoretically possible. But I can't see the advantage. Why would Mr. Holton fake his own death? Why would he want to disappear?"

"Maybe he wanted out of a bad marriage."

"Was it a bad marriage? Not for me to say. But really, I think divorce is so much easier, don't you? He'd have done very well in a divorce settlement. Very well indeed."

Mindful of my experience at Fresh Start, I didn't finish the drink, just to let it know who was boss. "Can I ask you a question? If you don't think Howard Holton is alive, why are you pursuing this suit against Fiona Darling?"

"I'm not pursuing anything or anyone, Mr. Hawkins. I'm simply representing Tasha. Her business is very important to my firm, we're inclined to indulge her a bit if necessary. Of course if Howard really is dead, as all the evidence suggests, and your Miss Darling put her name on a book he wrote, which is what we allege, that raises some interesting possibilities."

"Such as?"

"Oh, theft, collusion, fraud, to name a few. And possibly a motive to have Brant murdered, if he found her out."

It seemed silly, really, not to finish the drink. I didn't have to prove anything on that score. Good Kentucky bourbon, it was a sin to let it evaporate.

"Another?" Thurston said.

"Thanks, I'm fine. You were saying something about theft, collusion, and fraud. Sounds like the name of a law firm."

He smiled. "I've heard all the lawyer jokes, Mr. Hawkins. What's ten thousand lawyers at the bottom of the ocean? A good start."

"Yeah, well, the Sturne family going after Fiona is like shooting skeet with a SAM missile."

He chuckled, shook his head—he remained unimpressed with the fairness argument. "A lawsuit is not a game, Hawkins. Good sportsmanship doesn't count for much. You play by the legal rules but take whatever advantage you can. Tasha maintains that the book could only have been written by her husband. We've taken her word for that and proceeded accordingly."

"Do you think it matters now?" I said.

The lawyer glanced at the closed door. The weeping had stopped and now we could hear the murmur of female voices.

"That will be up to Tasha," he said. "She tends to be . . . whimsical."

"Any idea who might have wanted Brant dead?"

Thurston's smile was grim and worldly. "You were in that room of his, what do *you* think?"

"I think he was a sick puppy, but what does that have to do with it?"

"Maybe nothing," he said. "Maybe everything. Brant Sturne liked rough trade, Mr. Hawkins. Maybe the trade got a little *too* rough."

"You're saying a male prostitute killed him?"

"Let me put it this way: it wouldn't have been the first time he invited a shady character into the family suite. All he had to do was telephone one of the so-called escort services. Look 'em up in the Yellow Pages. From what Tasha told me, he knew what numbers to dial. In New York it got so bad she had to alert hotel security."

"But if he was about to entertain a prostitute, why invite us over?"

The lawyer leered.

"You tell me," he said. "You're the fun couple."

18

e'd been eating a lot of take-out lately, and that night was no exception. From the Sturne Royal we made a short detour to a pizza joint on Newbury Street, one of those down-in-the-basement places. Meg did the honors and came back with a large pepperoni, filling the van with the hot scent of bread, tomatoes, and spices.

"I feel bad for Tasha," Meg said as I swung the van into the parking garage adjacent to our building.

"Come on."

"No, I mean it. I got the impression she hasn't a friend in the world. Not a real friend. The lawyer was just there because he's on retainer, that's obvious."

"Meg," I said, wheeling into the elevator. "She's a trillionaire or something. And she's trying to ruin your pal Fiona."

"Yeah. I tried to keep that in mind. But Brant getting killed has thrown her for a loop. Maybe she didn't much *like* her brother, but she did love him, you know? Their parents died young, they had to rely on each other. Now she's more or less alone in the world."

"So money doesn't buy happiness, huh? I better call Russ, tell him to stop the presses."

"Jack, have a little sympathy."

"After we eat I'll have sympathy. Makes a good dessert, in small portions."

There are only three units on the top floor of our building, so we rarely bump into our neighbors in the hallway. Rarer still do we find uninvited guests waiting outside our door.

"Larry?"

Sergeant Detective Sheehan dropped his cigarette in a foyer ashtray littered with identical butts. "Where ya been? I thought you came home at night like normal people."

Meg made waving motions at the smoke. Sheehan ignored her, screwed his face up into a cocky grin. "Hey, pizza! My fave."

I started unlocking and said, "To what do we owe this dubious honor?"

"You think I don't know what dubious means? That you could sneak that in?"

"Save the aggrieved act," I said, pushing open the door. "Two slices, that's all you get."

Detective Sheehan accepted a beer with the pizza. Meg had seltzer. The beer looked good but I made myself chase the hotel drinks with strong black coffee. There are those who will say I was supplanting one drug with another, caffeine for alcohol. I urge them to form a liaison with Muffin the evaluator, and seek their own level in the New Puritan Hell.

Yes, I was feeling grumpy. Not, mind you, hungover.

"You been to see the sister, huh?" Sheehan said. His teeth were always giving him trouble and he chewed slowly and carefully.

"She called, granted us an audience."

"Like the Pope, huh?"

"Does the Pope own a chain of hotels?"

"Sure he does," Sheehan said. "Are you kidding? And they all got Pope on a Rope soap, too."

"Larry, I thought you were Catholic."

"I'm Irish Catholic. Gimme an Irish pope and I won't make jokes. Seriously though, did Mrs. Holton name any suspects?"

"Not exactly."

I told him about the "rough trade" theory, that Brant apparently had a history of telephoning so-called escort services.

"Yeah, we're checking that out," Shcchan said. "Trouble is, there was a private phone line in there, the log would only show for long-distance calls. I know this Vice detective, he said he'd ask around. Only I gotta tell you, usually when we get a pross involved in a homicide, it's the pross who gets murdered. But hey, maybe this could be the exception."

Megan spoke up. "The theory stinks," she said. "Whoever killed Brant knew him. And I don't mean knew him for a ten-minute interval of passion."

Sheehan fiddled with the label on the beer bottle. "How do you figure?" he said.

"A john who got carried away and killed him would have fled the scene, not taken the time to rig up the velvet noose. Whoever did that knew Brant was obsessed with sexual asphyxia."

Sheehan was nodding. "That's the way I see it, too. We get our share of rough trade homicides—almost always it's a beating or a blade. They like the knife, they like the blood, they get real messy. This was too calculated for a bondage scene." He hesitated, coughed into his fist. "Also, there was no indication of, um, arousal, the victim."

It was fun, watching Sheehan get embarrassed in the company of a female. Where he came from— where he still lived, at least in his head—a man didn't discuss sex with a woman, except possibly in the act of intercourse, and even then rarely. Over the years his relationship to Megan had progressed from outright hostility to wary respect. Despite himself I think he valued her opinion, although it was not something he would have admitted.

Sheehan drained the beer and put a Lucky Strike in the corner of his mouth without lighting it. "Do me a favor?" he said. "This lady friend of yours that was seen near the victim's suite, if she contacts you, tell her to contact me."

"Is she a suspect?" Meg asked.

"Not yet. But I have a hunch she witnessed something, the very least. The longer she stays out there the worse it looks, get me?"

"Got you."

"Okay, there's one other thing, the reason I came by."

"I thought you came by to sleaze a pizza," I said.

Sheehan gave me his hard look, an expression he'd acquired on the mean streets of Chelsea. It still worked with punks and to a lesser extent it even worked with me.

"Hey," I said. "You're welcome. Have another slice. Go on, light up that cigarette. Need a beer?"

That got him chuckling and the hardness softened.

"This guy Margolis," he said. "You seen him? The guy with Fitzroy Security?"

"Couple days ago," I said. "His house in Winthrop."

"Yeah, we been out there, he's gone."

"You want to talk to him too, huh?"

A match flared and Sheehan chewed smoke. "Yeah, I do. But the thing is, he ain't reported into work."

"What?"

"I got it from his supervisor. Margolis ain't been heard from since yesterday afternoon. Which, I guess, is not like him. Also about two hours ago his car shows up in a tow yard, Revere. Been yanked from short-term parking out at Logan. At the International Terminal."

"Homicide located the car?" I said.

Sheehan shook his head. "Nah, that was the

Fitzroy people. They got a bug up their . . . excuse me, they're pretty worried about this Margolis guy. They sent a couple of men out to the tow yard, pop the trunk. Like they expected to find their boy inside."

"And?"

"Would I be asking you if they found him in there, the trunk? What it is, he's missing. And since this Fiona broad is missing too, it made me think. Like maybe he's tailing her. Except, see, if it was a tail he'd still be reporting in. Or that's what Fitzroy Security says."

Sheehan stood up, washed his hands in the kitchen sink, patted dry with a paper towel, and never missed a puff. "Who knows?" he mused. "Maybe we got us a hot romance. Gumshoe runs off with a mystery writer. Hey, Jack?"

"What?"

"You should write this down."

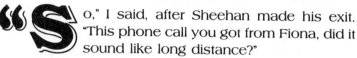

19

"So," I said, after Sheehan made his exit. "This phone call you got from Fiona, did it sound like long distance?"

Megan was cagey. "You can't tell nowadays."

"Meg, this is serious."

"Well . . . I didn't assume it was long distance, no."

After a long and fairly tumultuous day I should have been exhausted. Instead I was wheeling around the living room like a man on fire, trying to figure out exactly what it was about the whole situation that bugged me. And no matter how you tried to put it together, Brant and his sister, the Holton connection, it all came back to Fiona.

Quiet, sad, talented Fiona, who'd charmed us into helping her and then left us holding the bag.

"You know what I think?" I said. "I think she's in the area."

"Now Jack."

"She didn't come here," I said, making a turn around the coffee table. "She's not at the loft. What does that leave?"

"Two thousand motels," Meg said.

"Not to mention the bed and breakfasts," I said. "Not to mention one bed and breakfast in particular."

"Jack, you've no reason to think that—"

"Can't a guy have a hunch?" I said, snatching my winter jacket. "Haven't you ever heard of male intuition?"

"Jack, it would be better if you just—"

"Come on, Meg, the train is leaving."

Meg sighed, donned her parka. "Just remember," she said. "This is *your* idea."

*   *   *

Lynda Raven had her bookstore parking lot blocked off with barrels and planks. On the barrels, dripping in Day-Glo orange, the warning:

TRESPASSERS VIOLATED!

"Pretty subtle, huh?" I said.

"Well," Meg said, "this *is* Cambridge."

"One day soon she'll get herself a pit bull."

Getting into the spirit, Meg grinned and said, "No, something in the cat family. A leopard, maybe."

Meg got out, shifted a plank, and made room for the van. I parked next to a beat-up Volkswagen Beetle that looked as if it had been abandoned there in the mid-Sixties. After exiting the lift, I worked my way over muddy ruts in the parking lot, Megan at my side, not in any great hurry to disturb the irascible bookstore owner.

There was a warm front passing through and clouds rippled over the night sky, glowing with the lights of the city. Very atmospheric, fitting for an after-dark visit to The Raven's Nest. No doubt the squeaking sign over the entrance was Lynda's doing; she's prone to macabre touches, has been known to prop cadaver-like dummies in the window, as an enticement or warning, no one can be sure.

The street entrance was, no surprise, locked. Meg pushed the doorbell, but there was no answering gong inside.

"I think she switches it off when the store closes."

I backed into the street, looked up. "Lights on in Lynda's apartment. Lights on in the attic, too."

The rarely rented B&B rooms were on the attic level. Where Fiona and other writers had been given shelter. Where someone was clearly now in residence.

"Doesn't mean anything," Meg said. "Could be anybody up there. Another writer."

"Let's find out," I said, leading the way around to the side entrance. That too was locked. Where the doorbell had been, two wires protruded from the wood casing. "How's your arm?" I asked. "Can you get a rock through one of those windows?"

"Jack!"

"We're getting in there if we have to break in."

Meg banged her fist against the door while I shouted. After a while a figure came to one of the lighted windows, opened it.

"I've got automatic weapons!" Lynda announced. "I've got grenades!"

I rolled back out of the shadows, raised my hands. "We surrender!"

"Hawkins? Is that you? What the hell do *you* want in the middle of the night?"

"Lynda, it's not even ten o'clock."

"Don't tell me what time it is!" she shouted. "I *know* what time it is!"

Another ten minutes passed before she finally agreed to descend to ground level and let us in. I had to bump up over several stairs to get into her back hallway, and that contributed to my general irritation.

"Damn it Lynda, why'd you pry off the doorbell?"

"Didn't," she said. "It was stolen."

"Your *doorbell* was stolen?"

"What do you want, a polygraph test? *Yes*, it was stolen. You had to see me, you should have called first."

"I did," I said. "Your message was running."

From the back hall I rolled into the main room of the store. Lynda came along behind me and clicked on the lights. "What's the matter with this man?" Lynda demanded of Meg. "Has he gone completely round the bend?"

"He, um, thinks you're hiding Fiona."

Lynda wore a tailored kimono and sandals. In the subdued lighting she appeared almost childlike, a porcelain doll. Her voice, drenched in sarcasm, was entirely adult. Bette Davis in a bad mood.

"Hiding? Sorry to disappoint, Sherlock, but the lady is not here and if she *was* she wouldn't be hiding— she'd be my guest. And furthermore it seems to me that *you* are uninvited."

"You let us in," I pointed out.

"A technicality. And already I regret it."

"Look, I didn't mean to imply that Fiona is a fugitive or that you might be hiding her from the law, but she *is* wanted for questioning."

"Wanted?" Lynda's smile was something a blowtorch might have carved in ice. "As in 'Wanted' posters?"

"She happened to be seen in the vicinity of Brant Sturne's suite last night. At approximately the time he was murdered. Naturally the homicide detectives would like to ask her a few questions."

"Oh," she said. "Is that all? Turn her over to the men with the rubber hoses?"

"Worse that could happen, Larry Sheehan would blow smoke in her face. And I doubt he'd even do that."

Meg had taken a seat in the browsing room and was thumbing through a book. When I cleared my throat, indicating a need for backup, Meg smiled pointedly at me, pointedly at Lynda. Message received: this was my expedition, my argument, my problem. Meg was waiting out the war in her own little Switzerland.

"Who's on the third floor, Lynda?"

"None of your beeswax, Junior."

"I could have told Sheehan to put this place under surveillance," I said. "Maybe I should have."

"Is that a threat?"

"Come on, Lynda, is she up there? I've been chasing all over the city trying to help her out. Hell, we went all the way down to New York on her behalf. And now she won't even talk to us."

"Oh?" Lynda said, crossing her little arms. "Us?"

I glanced at Meg, who appeared to be deep into a new Jonathan Valin mystery. "Well, me in particular," I admitted.

Lynda sat down on the stairs, gathered the kimono around her legs. "Think about it," she said. "Consider this possibility: Maybe your assistance is not required here. Maybe Fiona doesn't *want* you messing around, making a lot of noise, attracting attention."

"Did she tell you that? Doesn't matter now, Lynda, this has gone beyond friendship or favors. Brant Sturne is dead and another man is missing."

Lynda's eyebrows went up. "What man?"

"A Fitzroy Security investigator. He had Fiona's place staked out. His car was found abandoned at Logan Airport."

"Oh." Clearly she wasn't interested, or didn't think it important.

"You have some other 'missing man' in mind?" I asked.

"I don't know what you're talking about."

"Does Fiona?"

"How would I know?"

"She's up there, isn't she Lynda?"

The sound of hurried footsteps came from the back hallway. Lynda smiled and said, "No, I don't believe she is."

Megan hadn't moved from her seat.

I swore, pushed hard for the back hallway. No one tried to stop me, no one offered to help. I got the back door open on my own, saw the beat-up Volkswagen backing out of the lot.

A streetlight hit the windshield, illuminating Fiona Darling behind the wheel. A moment later the taillights were fading down Mass. Ave. and I was starting to get really and truly pissed off.

20

It wasn't our first serious argument, of course, merely the first since we'd been married, and so took on a special significance, at least for Megan, who remembers everything, down to the color of the dress she wore for a sixth-grade recitation.

"It's so ridiculous," she said. "The idea that we're conspiring against you."

We were back home, after a noisy ride across the river. There had been no point in trying to follow Fiona—it takes me at least five minutes to get situated in the van, by which time she was long gone.

"I didn't use the word 'conspire.' I said that you and Fiona and Lynda had been doing things behind my back."

"Amounts to the same thing."

Meg, still wearing the green parka, threw herself on the couch. In the heat of the argument, midway down Memorial Drive, she'd started crying. That made her madder. Now her eyes were red and glittering and the tear-swollen pout was beginning to look like a permanent affliction.

"Are you denying that you knew she was there?" I said, trying to keep my voice at a reasonable level.

"I didn't know for sure."

"A sworn affidavit wasn't necessary."

"Jack, you're *so* sarcastic. You should hear yourself."

I pushed around the room. Concentrate on cooling down. Remember that this is the woman you love. Try to see things from her point of view.

"I'm out of the loop," I said. "Why can't you trust me?"

"It's not me, Jack. This isn't about me. Or you, for that matter."

"I hate the idea there are secrets between us."

"We can't share *everything*, Jack. It's just not possible between two human beings."

"I reject that argument."

"Fine," Meg said, bouncing to her feet. "Reject it. I'm going to bed."

I'd always wondered about the living room couch. It turned out to be quite comfortable. Not that I slept worth a damn. Every time I started to nod off a siren would wail, or some fool would burn rubber down Beacon Street, cheating the lights.

The other thing I discovered: If you listen hard enough in the dark, someone is always sobbing.

We made up over coffee. That is, we resumed speaking, treating each other with elaborate deference. By unspoken mutual agreement we did not mention Fiona Darling or the book or the murder or the fact that we had slept in separate beds.

"Looks like rain," I said. "Better take your umbrella."

"I left it at work."

"Take mine then."

"Thank you, I'll be fine."

I watched from the bedroom window as Megan Drew walked up Beacon Street. Trying to judge the state of her heart by the bounce in her step. Not much bounce, from what I could see, but what did that mean, really?

It meant I was afraid. Not afraid of losing Meg—it was merely an argument, passing showers in a mostly sunny relationship—but of losing the intimacy that had melded us together. An intimacy that made me feel like a whole man, despite my paraplegia. If the sharing ever stopped I would become a cripple again, that's what I feared most.

I drank too much coffee and then with sour, edgy nerves returned to my desk and booted up the word processor. I had a book to finish. The completed chapters, taken word by word, crawled like luminous worms across the screen. I couldn't make sense of it—who *were* these characters? They didn't seem to belong to me, not that day, not in that mood.

Parked in front of the slider, I stared out at the gray river, the MIT dome, the ebb and flow of slushy traffic on Storrow Drive. Above the Esplanade pigeons fought the wind, fluttering like broken kites against the sky.

April may be the cruelest month but March, let me tell you, March can be a bastard. I was feeling low enough to write bad poetry when Russ White called.

"We have another one, amigo."

"Russ? What are you talking about?"

"Just picked it up on the scanner. Officer responding to report of a body, vicinity the Fort Point Channel. The warehouse, Jack. Fiona's loft."

Strangely enough I was not surprised. My rational mind tells me that Fate is an abstract concept, a pattern we impose on an otherwise incomprehensible reality, but I arrived at the warehouse convinced that somebody I knew was dead.

There were two patrol cars on the street, lights flashing. Russ White, who'd had to fight his way through Government Center traffic, was just getting out of his Honda wagon, accompanied by a photographer.

"Any bets?" he said.

"Could be Jimmy Hoffa," I said. "Either him or Judge Crater."

The photographer, a skinny, big-eared kid, looked puzzled.

"Judge who?" he said.

"Old news," Russ said, taking the boy's arm. "Keep your distance, just try to get a shot before Homicide gets here. You get in too close, the uniforms will freak. So let the lens do the work."

"An intern," he confided. "Best I could do on short notice."

Having seen Russ White in action, I followed slightly behind, trying to blend in, although it's tough to be inconspicuous in a wheelchair. Russ, old pro that he is, didn't try to pull anything sleazy with the patrolmen who had responded to the report. You don't get to be a top crime reporter without carefully cultivating sources throughout the police department, from the commissioner's level on down. Contrary to the fictionalized stuff you see on television, a good journalist never gives lip to a cop—not if he wants to get the next story.

All four patrolmen were standing inside the warehouse, surrounding a heavyset forklift driver. The driver was using his hands as he talked, obviously excited. He kept pointing to the rear of the stall, where a man-sized lump lay under a canvas tarpaulin.

"Excuse me, officer." Russ introduced himself to the young cop who had detached himself from the group. "After you finish up here, could I get a statement from the responding patrol officers?"

"*The Standard,* huh? Wadda you know about this?"

"Only that a body was reported. We monitor the police bands."

"That a fact? Yeah, we got a body here, under the tarp. Guy found it when he moved a pallet of drums. All we can do, secure the scene, wait for the Homicide Unit. Gotta make sure nobody messes around," he added pointedly.

"Has Detective Sheehan been informed, do you know?"

The cop shrugged. "The Turret takes care of that. We just, um ascertained it's an actual dead person, not some bundle of rags."

"Sheehan would want to know about it," Russ told him in a confidential tone. "If you radio D Street and alert the Homicide Unit to notify Sheehan specifically, it can't do you any harm."

The cop looked suspicious. "Yeah?" he said.

"Cross my heart."

The cop shrugged, went back to his vehicle, returned a few minutes later. In the meantime the boy photographer had sidled into the storage bay and was clicking away without a strobe.

"From that angle all he can see is wadded-up tarpaulin," I said.

"It's a start," Russ said, keeping his voice low. "If he can't get anything better, we can run that with an arrow. 'Undercover Corpse' or 'Cold-Storage Killing.'"

"What makes you think it's murder, Russ? Could be somebody dropped dead on the job."

"And jumped under a tarp? Come on."

"A wino getting out of the cold. I happen to know this garage door was left unlocked."

Russ gave me a look. "Oh right," he said. "You paid a visit, looking for the lady. That's why you know about the door."

The young patrolman returned. "I gave 'em the message. They said Detective Sheehan was in court today, they'd beep him."

"You did the right thing," Russ assured him. "You made the stiff yet?"

The cop hesitated. "We're not supposed to say nothing until the detectives get here. They got to notify the family before they release the name, you know that."

"Sure," Russ said. "You can tell me the victim's gender, correct? Was it male?"

"You could a heard that on the scanner. So yeah, it's a guy."

"You got what, his wallet? Some ID?"

I said, "I hope it's not Ted Margolis."

The patrolman, his bland young face clouding with suspicion, turned to look directly at me for the first time. "You better tell me who you are, mister, and how come you know the victim."

"Damn," I said. "It *is* Margolis. Son of a *bitch*."

"You stay right here, mister," the cop said. "Detectives will want to talk to you."

Russ was giving me his grim-but-interested look. "Okay, we both knew he was missing and we both guessed right about the body. So what can you tell me about Margolis?"

I told him what little I knew. That Margolis was a retired Navy Intelligence captain who had made a second career with Fitzroy Security, that he was divorced. That he had seemed bright and personable and struck me as a canny investigator, not easily rattled by gunplay or surprise visits.

"Straight? I mean honest?"

"I only talked to him for half an hour, how should I know?"

"That was your impression though? A straight-shooter?"

"Yeah, that was my impression."

Larry Sheehan arrived twenty minutes later, dressed for court in a dove-gray overcoat and a new, custom-tailored suit. From the neck down he could have been a Milk Street bond salesman. "What're you lookin' at?" he said before turning to the patrolmen, who'd managed to secure coffee and donuts.

After chatting briefly with the uniforms, Sheehan took off the overcoat, loosened his tie, and lifted the corner of the tarp.

"Hawkins," he called out, "get your ass over here."

I rolled over. My hands felt weak and ineffectual as I gripped the rims. Sheehan lifted the tarp higher. "Can you make 'im?"

I made him. Lying on his side, arms folded across his chest, Margolis appeared to be sleeping, his head resting on a brown pillow. His mouth was slightly open. I blinked and the pillow was made of congealed blood.

Sheehan pulled the tarp back further, revealing a length of black iron pipe.

"Crushed the back of his head," he said. "I'll bet the poor bastard never saw it coming." He turned to me. "Wife? Family?"

"Divorced," I said. "That's all I know."

"The killer wacks 'im, drives the victim's car to the airport. Sound reasonable?"

"I suppose so."

"The big question. Does the killer get on the first plane out? Or take a cab back into the city? Any thoughts on that?"

"How should I know," I said.

"It would make a difference," he said, turning to give me the full bore of his cop eyes, "if you saw the suspect recently. You'd tell me, right? Right?"

"Take one glance at a victim, already you've got a suspect?"

Sheehan lowered the tarp, wiped his hands. A small scuff of dust showed on one knee, spoiling the crisp perfection of the new suit. "Yeah," he said. "The lady who lives upstairs here. You need a reason why she split in such a hurry, this fits the bill pretty good."

"Fiona," I said.

"Margolis tails her from the hotel, maybe he wants to ask her a couple questions, she's not in the mood. So, you seen her lately?"

Larry waited, not pushing.

"Yes," I said. "As a matter of fact I have."

It felt strange, cooperating with the police.

21

Home base for the Homicide Unit is in South Boston, on one of the alphabet streets that used to be snug at the top o' the lungs in many a shamrock bar and grill. A crowd-pleasing tune about being brought up on A Street, married on B Street—was it buried on C Street? I can't remember now, but the chorus was a rousing "Southie is my hometown!"

To those of us who *weren't* born on A Street the barely subliminal message was abundantly clear: if it ain't *your* neighborhood, pal, keep off the turf. Of course the sentiment of exclusion wasn't confined to good old Southie. There were similar echoes in East Boston, from the Charlestown Townies, in Dorchester, Roxbury, the North End (and the old West End before they tore it down), and in many of the surrounding cities. Larry Sheehan and his tenement toughs didn't need a song to stake out Chelsea—strangers got "the look," a kind of visceral glare that felt like a cold spike between the shoulder blades.

Sheehan, although still capable of wordless intimidation, played it cozy that day. Overhearing the conversation, you might have gotten the impression we were a couple of pals discussing an event of mutual interest. An event that just happened to be murder.

"So, she took off, huh? And you didn't follow?"

"Hey, I was at the back door, she was already exiting the parking lot. I'm not into high-speed chases, Larry, in case you haven't noticed."

He gave me the Sheehan eyeball and grinned.

"I never did, no. So what are you sayin', I oughta go see this Raven broad?"

"That's up to you. My impression, you could put Lynda on the rack she still wouldn't talk."

"The rack is in for repair," Sheehan said.

"Too bad."

"What's your reading on the lady, Jack? She a swinger?"

"Huh?"

He put his fists together and mimicked swinging a bat. "Miss Fiona Darling, she the hot-tempered type? Gets pissed at a nosy gumshoe, wacks him out?"

"I don't know, Larry. I wouldn't have thought so."

"But now you're not so sure?"

I shrugged. "I get the idea she's hiding something—or covering for someone. That doesn't mean she's a killer."

"No," Sheehan said doubtfully. "I suppose not."

"Any progress with Brant Sturne?"

He started to shake his head, then paused. Changed his mind about not telling me. "Some," he said. "The Crime Scene boys were in there, must have been twelve hours. Samples up the wazoo."

"Fingerprints?"

He shrugged. "Sure, you need a few? I got millions. We hadda print everybody on the staff, and that's only current. They come and go in the hotel business, right?"

"So what *did* you find?"

He hesitated. "This is for you, not your reporter friend, okay? But we got some really good fibers. Under the victim's fingernails and a few could be the same type clinging to his shirt, like he picked 'em up in a struggle. We sent 'em down to the FBI, they got a special lab there, does nothing but match fibers."

"Fibers are good," I said. "Unless the killer was smart enough to get rid of everything he was wearing."

"Which is why I don't want to read about this in the paper."

I zipped my lips.

"Good. Silence is golden."

"Larry, you know what's wrong here? You're too damn happy."

"What? I'm *happy?*"

"Which indicates to me you've got something better than fiber samples. You got, what, a match already? A suspect? You're about to make an arrest?"

Sheehan averted his eyes. "You're a weirdo, Hawkins. Must be all those books you write, your brain is twisted or something. Now you think you're a mind reader."

"Larry, I can smell it on you. You've got hard evidence. And it's not Fiona Darling, am I right?"

The eyes clicked back to me—once again he'd changed his mind. "It's not anybody we know. Not yet."

"Solid physical evidence," I said. "You got a blood sample, right?"

"Jack—"

"Am I right? Brant managed to scratch the killer and now you've got blood? Under his nails, maybe?"

Sheehan was laughing silently, shaking his head. "Close. What we got is actually better. We got stomach contents."

"What? From Brant—but how does that help?"

"Not Brant. In the bathroom. Somebody threw up in there, and they didn't get it all in the toilet, neither. So we got stomach enzymes and fluid and even a little blood."

"Damn," I said. "You've got DNA."

"Fucking right we do."

DNA matching was a recent forensic science breakthrough. The technique, developed in England, made it possible to "fingerprint" chromosomes, provided you had blood or body fluid to identify.

"All we need now is a suspect," Sheehan said. "I

can put 'im in the room, I can show fiber. Even this jerk DA we got couldn't screw it up."

"You're doing good work, Detective."

"Matter of fact, we are."

"Congratulations."

"So," he said. "You hear from the lady, you'll let me know?"

Back home there was a message on the machine. Russ White sounding excited.

Call me, man. Stuff is happening.

He picked up on the first ring.

"No comment," I said.

"Who asked?"

"You want to know what did I say to Detective Sheehan and what did he say to me. The substance of our conversation."

Russ barked a laugh. "Sure, you wanna tell me, fine. But that's not why I called."

"You miss me," I said.

"That's it. You're my favorite companion, it comes to viewing a dead body."

"I guess it wasn't you who left a message."

"Don't get huffy on me, Hawkins. You get huffy, you don't get to meet Mary Beth Maxam."

"Mary Beth who?"

"Maxam," he said, his voice going soft. "She's this really terrific . . . she's this financial reporter who's been checking out the money angle on the Sturne family. She came up with some pretty interesting material."

"You've got my attention," I said. "Tell you what, how about if you and Mary Beth Maxam stop by after work."

"Your place? Drinks or dinner?"

"What the hell," I said. "Both."

22

Megan was a good sport about it, considering.

"I only bought for the two of us," she said as she unpacked the groceries.

"This could be important," I said.

"I'm really not in the mood."

"I'll give 'em the heave right after coffee."

"Most wives, their husbands spring unannounced dinner guests, it goes very badly."

"You're not most wives."

Meg eyed the clock. "There's shrimp in the freezer. I could fake a scampi."

"I love a fake scampi."

"This woman," she said. "Is she involved with Russ?"

"See?" I said. "Already you're dying to know."

Russ White was a confirmed bachelor, but if he'd had a daughter, Mary Beth Maxam could have passed for her. Dark red hair cut in short bangs, freckles, a perky smile, that was my first impression. Surely this obvious schoolgirl couldn't be a financial reporter? Financial reporters wore half-rims and squinted a lot, or else they looked like bookies—come to think of it, a lot of bookies wear half-rims and squint a lot. Which proves my point, sort of.

"I know, I know," Russ said, helping her off with her coat. "She's hideously young."

"Shut up about my age," Mary Beth said pleasantly.

Her voice, at least, was mature.

"I've read all of your Casey books," she added. "They're fabulous."

Mature, I decided, and wise beyond her years. As Mary Beth headed into the kitchen to introduce herself to Megan, Russ whispered, "Whatever you do, don't offer her milk and cookies."

"I'll try to remember."

"It's the flawless complexion and the size-five dress," he added, keeping his voice low. "Really she's a graduate student. One of our work-study kids."

"Ah."

"You keep saying 'ah.' What am I, a doctor?"

"Dr. Russ," I said. "Pediatrician."

"Please. Remember what it was like to be that young."

"I was never that young," I said.

Russ was a beer drinker. Mary Beth opted for a glass of white wine. We sat around the kitchen and watched Megan chop garlic while the rice steamed.

"Frozen shrimp," Meg said, by way of apology.

"The best kind," Mary Beth said brightly. "They ice 'em down on the boat, so what they call 'fresh' here in Boston means it's been thawed out at least once."

Mary Beth, as it turned out, had worked her way through college waiting tables at Legal Seafood, and knew whereof she spoke.

"How did Russ rope you into checking out the Sturne family finances?"

Mary Beth laughed. She looked just a little bit like the girl on the Vermont Maid syrup bottle, except that her hair wasn't woven into braids. "Rope me? I *begged* for the story—you figure rich-kid murder, kinky sex, it has book-length possibilities. True crime stuff is hot right now."

I cleared my throat. "Maybe Russ has the same idea, hey Russ?"

Russ opened his mouth but it was Mary Beth who spoke first: "We already settled it. If the stuff I uncovered is a factor, we'll collaborate on any book deal."

Russ nodded sheepishly. "She does amazing research," he said.

"Thanks, hon."

She patted his hand and then I knew: Russ White was smitten.

"Take your places," Meg said over the sizzling fry pan.

The scampi, no surprise, was perfect, served with Meg's Cajun-style rice (I know they call it "dirty," but really, what an unpleasant thought) and a slightly sweetened, okra-corn combo that required the quaffing of additional beers to clear the palate.

You don't linger over a meal like that, so the coffee had been served before I looked up from my plate and got down to the business of pumping Mary Beth.

If you'll pardon the expression.

"So," I said. "What did you know and when did you know it? And remember you're under oath."

Mary Beth turned to Russ and said, "He's kidding, right?"

"Yeah, Jack's a great kidder."

"Tell you what," Mary Beth said, her eyes brightening. "The same deal applies to you. If any of my research stuff is a factor in solving the crime, you agree to cooperate by giving me—us—any source material we may need to complete a book."

"You interview us, we tell all, is that the idea?"

"That's the idea."

"Assuming that Brant Sturne's killer is brought to trial."

"Correct," she said. "The way it works with a true crime book, it's best to work backwards from a jury verdict. That way you're indemnified against libel."

The coffee slipped down the wrong way and I

coughed. Russ tried to pat me on the back but I waved him off. A little caffeine was good for the lungs. When I'd got my breath back I grinned at Mary Beth and said, "You've got it all figured out, huh?"

"I'm trying," she said. "And I've got some great stuff. Kinky sex is good as far as it goes—I mean as a tease to interest the readers—but all really interesting crimes have a money angle."

"And this does?"

"Let me put it this way. There's tens of millions of dollars at stake here. I'm not sure how it ties into Brant Sturne's murder. But even if it doesn't, it makes great background material."

Mary Beth went on to explain that Sturne International was "closely held." That is, although it was legally incorporated, all of the stock was owned or controlled by a relatively small number of shareholders. The largest blocks were controlled by Tasha, Brant, and Tasha's husband, Howard Holton.

"Wait a minute," I said. "You mean Howard Holton owned millions of dollars of Sturne International?"

"Not quite. And that's where it gets interesting. Tasha wanted her husband to participate in the family business—that is, attend board meetings with her. Sturne itself is run by a staff of professional managers, the board mostly rubber-stamps management decisions. But in any case, Tasha assigned her husband the proxy vote from a family trust."

"So he *didn't* own the stock."

"No. But he could *vote* as if he did. And if Tasha died first, the proceeds of the trust would go to her husband."

"Nothing for Brant?"

"Brant had his own block of stocks. And notice I said the *proceeds* of the trust, not the trust itself. Had Tasha died first, her husband would have had a secure income for as long as he lived, but upon *his* death the block of stocks would go to her heirs. Keeping control in the family. Presumably Brant would have been first in line."

"Can I ask you a question, Mary Beth?"

"Sure."

"How did you get this information?"

She hesitated, glanced at Russ, who nodded. "I have this friend," she said. "She's a CPA with one of the Big Eight."

"She audits the Sturne books?"

"No. But *she* has a friend—a boyfriend—who works for another big accounting firm, and he had access to certain information. I, um, got copies of the last few annual reports, as well as quarterly statements and the minutes of quite a few board meetings."

"Is it legal to get hold of that stuff?"

"It's not *illegal*. It would be if we were planning a hostile takeover, say, or had some kind of contractual relationship to Sturne International that could be improved by our knowledge."

When she got going, Mary Beth's speech went from a canter to a full gallop. I found myself pausing to rein her in. Money matters are not my strong point; it takes a while for me to absorb financial information.

"So," I said. "What exactly did you find out? What's the big money angle?"

"Two things," she said with a grin. "Death and parking."

"I thought it was 'death and taxes.'"

"Parking," she said. "Remember the scandal when the new hotel was being built? All kinds of hanky-panky with the building inspectors and the zoning board?"

"Sure. Couple of political hacks got fired. A few others pled to corruption charges. Lots of smoke and noise but really a fairly minor political shake-up, par for the course in this city."

"Right," she said. "Minor shake-up for the politicians. But in the middle of all that mess the new hotel lost the option on a parking facility. For a while they leased rights from a privately owned garage. That expired last fall and the garage refused to renew and now they have *no* parking. Forty-story hotel with no parking? It's gotta hurt."

"We noticed," Megan said. "Remember, Jack?"

"I do," I said. "But what has this got to do with a death? You said death and parking."

"Right. The board was set to vote on it last summer—putting up thirteen million dollars to buy the private garage outright. That's about twelve mil over appraised value."

"Wow," I said.

"Wow," Mary Beth echoed. "And then Howard Holton died or disappeared or whatever he did, and so he wasn't there to vote his proxy, rubber-stamp the purchase and sale agreement. The decision has been put off until the courts decide who gets his proxy vote."

"He didn't leave it to Tasha?"

"He did leave it to her. But his death is in dispute, remember? Largely because Tasha refused to believe he was dead. As a result, the board has not taken a vote since her husband vanished. Or drowned, or ascended into heaven, or whatever he did."

Whatever Howard Holton had done, he hadn't ascended into heaven, I decided. Possibly he'd extricated himself from hell.

Megan, for her part, was being very quiet. Making no comment about how Fiona Darling might or might not be involved in financial shenanigans with Howard Holton. For all our forced politeness there was still a distance between us, a sense that certain things could not be shared.

"Let me see if I've got this right," I said. "Thirteen million dollars was going to change hands. Then a man went fishing and didn't come back and so the transfer of funds hasn't happened yet. Is that about it?"

Mary Beth looked disappointed. "Oh it's much more complicated. The struggle within the board. The legal implications. Not to mention the effect on a multi-million-dollar enterprise like the Sturne Royal Boston."

"But in essence, that's what happened?"

"Well . . . yes."

I knew what she was thinking. Five or six nice juicy chapters of financial intrigue reduced to a couple of plain declarative sentences. A man goes fishing and a whole world collapses.

"So," I said. "The question is, who owns the garage? Who gets the thirteen mil? Is that the question?"

"That's the question," Russ said.

"That's *still* the question," Mary Beth said. "Got any ideas?"

23

You're buying, right?"

"Natch," I said.

We were in a fancy burger joint on Boylston, a current favorite with Fitzy because they hand-cut the french fries and topped the cheeseburgers with thick slices of Cabot sharp cheddar. This was a late lunch and quite possibly not his first of the day—Fitzy has been fighting his weight recently, but he always seems to go down in the first round, kay-oed by carbohydrates.

"Well," I said after we placed our orders. "Tell me she's got a sordid past. Some deep dark secret we can trade for access to her files."

Fitzy gave me his Cheshire cat grin and shook his head.

"Dream on," he said. "The lady is a saint. No malpractice suits, not even an unpaid parking ticket."

Finian X. Fitzgerald and I go way back. We skipped out of Boston Latin on many a spring day and headed for the Fenway Park bleachers. It was a buck a seat then, and tough guys with valid ID's would sell you a cup of warm Narragansett for two-bits above retail. We chased the same girls without coming to blows, palled around in college (B.U. before Long John Silber began spouting his reactionary rhetoric) and then for a time drifted our separate ways, he to Suffolk Law (nights) and I into a soft civilian job with the Boston Police Department.

Part of the drift was on account of Marge, my first wife, who found Fitzy abrasive. When I was reborn on wheels Marge opted out for life in California with a perfectly decent computer programmer whose name I can't seem to recall, ever. Fitzy handled the divorce as amicably as possible but Marge didn't think he should have handled it at all. She has her point of view. I simply make the point that Finian X. Fitzgerald is not abrasive, he just has certain irritating facets, which is a very different thing.

"To Dr. Helen Foster," he said, lifting a water glass. "Paragon of the medical profession."

"So," I said. "A shrink is obliged to protect patient confidentiality even if the patient is presumed dead?"

"Matter of fact, yes. Not obliged, exactly—you could debate the point—but the legal privilege usually holds."

"Drat," I said. "Double drat."

"There are, of course, one or two exceptions. For instance if said doctor has prior knowledge that his or her patient is about to commit a criminal act. The same goes for a lawyer defending a client—the privilege doesn't extend to knowledge of a future criminal act."

"How about potential?"

Fitzy waggled his burly red eyebrows. "Potential what?"

"The potential to be violent. Say a shrink diagnoses a patient as capable of great violence. Is she obliged to warn the police?"

"Oh," he said, his gaze swiveling to the waitperson, who arrived bearing a variety of cholesterols on a bright orange tray, "that kind of potential. The answer is 'probably not.' First place, expert testimony varies as to the definition of a psychopathic state—by psycho do you mean the raving lunatic, or the person with delusions who still manages to function on some level? The person who *thinks* about violence or the one who never thinks but simply acts? The presumption of innocence is not based on having an innocent state of mind. And a potential killer is innocent until he actually *commits* the crime."

"What about these crazies they round up wherever a president or a pope is appearing in public?"

"Either the crazy has made a threat—which is in violation of the law—or they have to let him go. That's legally. I'm not saying the Secret Service boys always stick within the law."

"But you're saying I should?"

"Should what?"

"Stay within the law."

"Absolutely," Fitzy said, tenderly lifting the plump burger from the plate. "Abso-positively. I would never counsel a client to break the law. Or a friend, for that matter."

We ate. Fitzy insisted on apple pie.

"An incomplete meal is bad for the health," he said. "And I am *very* health conscious."

"Any suggestions?" I said.

"Not so heavy on the ketchup," he said, and proceeded to finish my portion of fries while we waited for the pie.

"This is not helpful. It's possible this woman knows the identity of a murderer. There's even the possibility that she's involved in a financial swindle."

"What do you want me to say?"

"I figure she's in your neighborhood, you might know something we could use against her. Find a way to make her talk."

"Let's get something straight, Jack. The drying-out joint is in the South End, but the good doctor practices in Cambridge."

"But I saw her at Fresh Start."

"Two days a week for group therapy sessions.

Most of her business is across the river, consulting psychiatrist for a medical clinic."

"Ah ha," I said.

"I don't like the sound of that."

The pie arrived. I let Fitzy have both pieces. Figuring keep on his good side, you never know when you might need a good lawyer.

24

I began to feel in need of medical attention at exactly 4:29 P.M. That's when I rolled through recently renovated Harvard Square, heading for the Charles Medical Complex. At first glance the square looks much the same as it did in the bad old days when Fitzy and I quaffed exotic foreign beers in the Wursthaus or succumbed to midnight munchies at Elsie's. Skinny, wild-haired Fitzy playing with the stoned hipsters who pitched games of five-minute street chess—well, you had to have been there. And it helps to know that Fitzy played chess like checkers, leapfrogging his pawns and driving the intelligentsia to distraction.

The chess hustlers are still there, but the street people no longer have that furtive, underground look. Times have changed, even in Cambridge. We're in the Nineties now and Purple Microdot sounds more like a hot software firm than a once-popular hallucinogen.

So much for nostalgia. I had crimes to commit.

The Charles Medical Complex was a new, five-story office building. According to the listing in the lobby, Dr. Helen Foster shared office space with a group of family practitioners—the resident shrink, as it were.

A man on crutches held the elevator for me. I could tell by the gleam in his eye that he viewed my condition as a challenge—seek a cure and fling away the crutches. When the doors closed Mr. Crutches kept his face averted and then got off on the third floor. I was headed all the way to the top.

My plan, such as it was, had been based on this

premise: that the suite of offices occupied by Helen Foster and her associates would not be likely to employ an all-night watchman. They'd leave security to the building owner, and the Charles Medical Complex guards, like low-paid security stiffs the world over, would make a round or two to check that doors were locked and then retire to play cards, read, or sleep. Leaving a window of opportunity for any individual clever enough to secrete himself inside before closing.

That was my plan. At this hour most of the foot traffic was moving in the opposite direction; the lame, the halt, and the hypochondriac were streaming out of various offices, vacating the building. Dr. Foster's suite was no exception. When I rolled in the waiting area was almost deserted.

"Excuse me?"

There were several young receptionists tidying up data entry behind the counter. "Yes, sir?"

"I have an appointment with Dr. Feldman."

"Dr. Feldman? I'm afraid you're in the wrong office." Without looking up from her computer screen she added, "Dr. Feldman is on the fourth floor. This is five."

"This is five? It can't be."

A small laugh. All I could see was the top of her head behind the high, protective counter, the ambient glow of the screen. "Just go back to the elevator, sir. Punch number four. You'll be fine."

"May I use the bathroom first? It's an emergency."

"Um, do you need any help?"

"No, I can manage."

"Just down this hall," she said with evident relief, "first door on the left."

I was in sight of the twin doors to the rest rooms when footsteps came up behind me. Quick footsteps. Bearing Satchel Paige's advice in mind, I didn't risk a look back. And a good thing, too, because passing on my left, briefcase in hand, her eyes focused in the middle distance, was Dr. Helen Foster.

My breath caught in my throat. As luck would have it, the good doctor kept briskly on, her athletic stride eating up yards of hallway before she turned a corner and vanished from view.

A close call—and it would be several hours more before I realized just *how* close.

Pine scent. There was more pine scent in that one small closet than in all the woods of Maine—and I was in there long enough to become a human air freshener.

According to my calculations, staff and patients should have been gone by five-thirty at the latest, but several rather noisy types hung on until well after six. What's the world coming to when young office workers ignore the temptations of afterhour fraternization and stay late to catch up?

Sitting in the dark with nothing to do but eke out the minutes, my thoughts kept returning to Ted Margolis. What, exactly, had he admitted in our brief conversation? Although he'd left me with the impression that Fitzroy Security had been retained by Tasha's law-firm, he'd never actually said so. Had he intentionally misled me about the identity of his client? And if so, why?

At the time Tasha's interest in Fiona had seemed obvious. Now I wasn't so sure. What if Brant Sturne had hired Fitzroy Security to investigate Howard Holton's death? It made a kind of strange and twisted sense, the more I thought about it. Brant had come to Boston convinced that Howard was alive. What had given him that idea? A call from the author himself? Or a report from a certain Fitzroy Security investigator?

I didn't expect to find answers to those specific questions in Dr. Foster's files. The best I could hope for was some clue as to Howard Holton's behavior. Had he been a secret psycho, struggling with murderous impulses, capable of staging his own death? And what of Fiona Darling? Did they have more than an alcohol addiction in common? Was there a Bonnie and Clyde relationship there, the woman urging the man on to violence, sharing the thrill of duplicity, possibly of murder?

As Holton's shrink, Helen Foster had to know a lot more than she'd admitted to, and with people dying I couldn't let her fine sense of professional ethics stand in the way of exposing a killer.

That's what you tell yourself when you're hiding in the dark, about to engage in felony. Eventually the happy chattering ceased. There were mumbled goodbyes, the click of a door, a welcome silence.

I was about to exit the closet when the janitorial service arrived. Loud, bantering male voices, the sudden drone of a vacuum cleaner. And where was yours truly hiding? That's right, put a star on your forehead, the janitorial closet. Which didn't lock from the inside.

Grabbing the doorknob, I held on with both hands. Just in time, too, because almost immediately footsteps came thumping along—the damn fool was whistling—and the knob was being forced from the other side.

Tug. Tug. Left. Right. I squeezed.

"Hey Lou, we got a key to this? Huh? I think it's jammed."

Footsteps thumping away. I emptied my lungs, took a deep breath of pine-scent saturated air. A herd of footsteps returning.

"So go ahead wiseguy, *you* try it."

Lou, if that was his name, had considerable

strength. I felt my wrists twisting, losing leverage. Abruptly he let go.

"Ah, fuck it. Splash some water around the johns, it'll look like we hit 'em. I'll finish the rug work and then we're out of here."

The other voice said, "I could, you know, bust the lock."

"Are you nuts? You wanna toilet brush that bad, you'd bust a lock?"

"You're the boss."

"And don't you forget it. Get a move on, we got three more units this floor. Hit 'n' run, buddy boy."

The vacuuming persisted for another twenty minutes. I was compelled to hang on to that slippery doorknob, on the off chance that the enthusiastic toilet-scrubber would give it one more try.

When I emerged into the dim light of the corridor, the clean-up crew was gone. Air wafting through the heating system tainted the relative silence with a soft, humming quality that raised the small hairs on the back of my neck.

I was an intruder here, a criminal.

The door to Dr. Foster's office was, I soon enough discovered, unlocked. I reached into the storage pouch on my chair and withdrew a small flashlight. A quick scan, keeping the flashlight beam beneath the level of the windows, revealed a modestly sized desk and three upholstered chairs—no couch, do any shrinks still use a couch?—arranged for comfortable consultation. Very cozy. Bookcases lined one wall, file cabinets another.

I headed directly for "H" and immediately ascertained that the cabinets were locked.

In the movies your amateur sleuth will pick the lock with a handy paperclip in less than ten seconds. My personal reality is much less cinematic. I wasted thirty minutes searching Foster's desk for the key. Found notepads, a calculator, several expired appointment books, a gross of No. 2 pencils, a drawer devoted entirely to unpaid parking tickets, stationery, a screwdriver set, and enough paper clips to strangle a medium-sized bureaucracy.

No keys.

Paper clips were never an option. I settled for a small screwdriver and gouged at the lock. Got a bigger screwdriver and pried until the tongue snapped. Dynamite would have been neater. Holding the flashlight in my teeth, I flipped through the files. Haber, Hanes, Hartnett, Henderson, Hickelstem, and yes, there it was, *Holton, Howard H.*

The jacket was empty.

I pawed through files on either side, hoping that it had somehow been misfiled. No chance. I had a vision, right then, of Helen Foster striding along, briefcase in hand, heading back to her office. Back to collect the Howard Holton file? What for, bedtime reading?

More likely my little subterfuge at her South End clinic had alerted Foster to police interest in her client. Maybe she'd put the file in a more secure location or handed it over to a lawyer for safekeeping. Or some *other* interested party had got here before me.

Would Foster have done the same for her file on Fiona Darling—if in fact she *had* been treating Fiona? What the hell. By now I had practice in busting the file locks.

Come on, Fiona, be there.

This time there was not even an empty file jacket. There was no trace that Fiona had ever been under Helen Foster's care. *Nada.* Inspiration struck right about then: try the appointment book, you shmuck. If Helen of Cambridge has been treating Fiona, the proof will be there in her appointment book.

Having ransacked the desk for file keys, I knew right where the appointment books were kept. Top right-hand drawer. The good doctor favored the day-book style, lacking a cross index for client names. With the flashlight propped on a dictionary, I started in January of the previous year.

The first entry for Howard Holton was in March. Tuesday afternoon. No other information, just his name in a time slot. I flipped to the next week and found him there again in the same time slot.

Humming "Tuesday Afternoon," the classic Moody Blues tune, I flipped through the weeks and months and there he was, like most working novelists, a creature of habit. Tuesday was shrink day. And this raised another question—with all the psychiatrists in Manhattan, why would he choose to be treated in the Boston area? Was he making it a two-for-one deal, shuttling up to meet his doctor *and* his mistress?

Holton had disappeared into the Nantucket surf on the second weekend in July. The Tuesday before he had had his usual appointment with Dr. Foster.

No other appointments in July had been scheduled. I had to think about that for a bit, tipping the facts around, looking for an angle. Did no further appointments indicate that he had *intended* to disappear? Or was the answer simply that it was more difficult to commute from the island of Nantucket than from the island of Manhattan?

I flipped ahead into September and there he was, back to his regular Tuesday time slot. That got my heart beating fast enough to make me feel light-headed, almost giggly. I had the proof in firm black penmanship that Howard Holton was alive and well enough to see his favorite shrink a month after he was supposed to have died.

Ditto for October through December. The man never missed. By now there was no surprise in opening the book for the current year and finding that Tuesday still belonged to Howard Holton. He was in there every week, right up to the present.

I put the appointment books in my lap and went to look for a photocopy machine. Found it in an alcove by the reception desk. I had my finger on the button when the door opened and the lights came on.

"Don't move," a big cop said.

Cops tend to come in pairs. They were both pointing guns at me. I didn't move. I didn't breath.

"That's him," said Helen Foster, coming up behind them. "That's the lying son of a bitch."

25

egan Drew was so mad she was crying. Unfortunately her anger was not directed at the cops who'd arrested me, or Dr. Foster, who'd insisted that charges be preferred, or at Finian Fitzgerald, who'd come to bail me out.

"You stupid, stupid man," she said, holding her arms straight down at her side, fists gone white with clenching. "How could you?"

'Sometimes you have to do the wrong thing," I said. It was, of course, exactly the wrong thing to say.

It was midnight and we were on Thorndike Street, just outside the courthouse. My van, if it hadn't been towed by now, was on the other side of the city. I'd had four entertaining hours in the company of the Cambridge Police Department, to a man unimpressed with my contacts on the Boston cops. Visitors may consider Cambridge a quaint neighborhood of Boston, but the local constabulary have little regard for the "hotshots" on the other side of the river. This was, as they kept reminding me, a whole 'nother county, pal. Detective Sullivan? Never heard of 'im.

"Should I leave you two alone?" Fitzy was saying.

"Don't," Megan said. "I might strangle the son of a bitch."

Fitzy scratched his head, made a face. "Hmmm, this is pretty awkward. I better take you both home, that sound okay?"

"Perfect," Meg said. "Just perfect."

I rode in the front with Fitzy, who stowed my chair in the trunk. Meg perched on the rear seat, radiating tension. The short ride back into the city was a study in silence. Fitzy had recovered enough of his poise to be whistling "On the Street Where You Live" as he unpacked my wheels and brought them around to the passenger side.

"I'd *love* to come up for a nightcap, shoot the breeze with you two lovebirds," he said, "but Lois is waiting up. So I'll take a rain check."

Meg gave Fitzy a glum nod, cutting me out, then walked swiftly into the lobby. The door closed behind her.

"Funny," Fitzy said, glancing up at our building, "doesn't *look* like a doghouse."

Meg was in her chair in the living room, legs crossed, arms crossed, closing herself off. I rolled inside, took off my jacket, announced that I was about to pour a very strong drink.

"Care to join me?" I asked.

Ignoring the offer, Meg said, "I came home from work, you weren't here."

"I was out burglarizing. Is that a word, burglarizing?"

"No note. No phone call. Just gone. What was I supposed to think?"

"Megan," I said, lifting up a glass of Jameson Irish whiskey large enough to have gotten me into Dropkick Murphy's, even in the old days. "I didn't intend to get caught. I figured in, out, be home by seven, the latest."

"I thought . . . it came to mind that, you know, that something bad had happened."

"Something bad *did* happen. You're married to a potential felon."

"I mean *really* bad. It's not like you to take off without letting me know. You leave a note when you go down to the corner for a paper."

"I didn't come back here. I went directly to jail, do

not pass go. And I'm sorry if I gave you a fright. That wasn't what I had in mind."

Meg sighed, reached for the bottle. I was all agoggle. Megan Drew with a stiff drink, this was a first.

"You may want to dilute that with a little water," I suggested.

"Guess what kind of day I had," she said, taking the Jameson straight.

"I said I'm sorry about giving you a scare. And I meant it."

"Harold Standish came back today," she said, "and today he fired me."

"*What?*"

"Fired. F-I-R-E-D. Also known as canned, terminated, let go, bounced."

"That son of a bitch."

Meg drank deeply. "He felt he had to make an example of me," she said. "He'd been giving it a lot of thought, down there in the Caribbean. It was painful as heck, a most unpleasant task, but he'd asked Mary Kean to do it and she'd refused and when he suggested leaving a note on my desk Mary insisted he do it himself or else *she'd* walk."

"Megan—"

"You know the best part, Jack? He did it over the phone. He actually left the building and went over to one of his clubs and phoned from there."

"But why?"

"They're going to sue. No kidding this time. No stern letters from the big bad law firm, just a statement of fact. And so of course Harold Standish felt he had to make an example. Show the rest of the staff what happens to naughty editors."

"That slimey son of a bitch."

"I know," Meg said. "You never liked him."

"Now I'm *really* sorry I wasn't here when you got home."

Megan poured another drink.

"You may want to cut that with a little water. Smooth as it is."

"What happened between us, Jack? That you'd do a thing like that without telling me?"

Waiting for bail, I'd given that some thought. "Ted Margolis," I said. "He gets his head bashed in, Fiona is a prime suspect, and you didn't want to hear about it. That made me angry. Then I realized you were keeping something back—that you had a reason to believe Fiona was completely innocent."

"Maybe I do," she said. "Have a reason."

"That's the point," I said. "We've started having secrets."

"That's not fair."

"I agree," I said. "But you shut me out and I wanted to find a way to get back in."

"So you get yourself arrested? What kind of crazy plan is that? What does it prove?"

"Getting popped wasn't part of the plan," I said. "And it doesn't prove anything, except that I'm not a very skilled criminal. The doctor saw me, figured I was up to no good. Came back with the cops and caught me red-handed. As the saying goes."

Meg, always a quick learner, was now able to down the whiskey without shuddering. She did so and poured again. "And this all happened because that investigator died, right?"

"Was killed."

"Killed, then. You feel what, guilty because this guy you met once gets himself killed?"

"Murdered," I said. "That's much the better word. You can get killed walking into traffic. Murder is much more specific."

"Well, do you?"

"Feel guilty? No, I don't think so. Dumb is what I feel. Stupid. For believing all those lies."

"Ah," Meg said, cradling her glass. "Now we're getting to it. You think I lied to you."

"Nope," I said. "Not you. Unless you mean lied by omission, not telling me where she was. No, I refer to Fiona's lies. She *has* been lying, at least to me, hasn't she?"

Megan was silent, not looking at me. "I don't know that for a fact," she said at last, keeping her voice small.

"Fiona insisted that Howard Holton was dead," I said. "He's not. I found him tonight."

When I told her about the appointment books she reacted by draining the Jameson like a dose of medicine. "Oh God," she said, gasping. "What a crazy world."

"You knew?"

Meg took a deep breath. When she spoke again the whiskey was thick in her voice. "Knew the sick-*eye*-atrist'd have *something* in those files. Didn't know what, 'zactly. Only guesstimate."

"I didn't see the actual files," I reminded her. "I still don't know what Howard Holton is being treated for."

"Alk-haul," Meg said, and then giggled.

"More than alcohol. No man fakes his own death just to kick a booze habit. Or kills two other men just to cover the fact that he's still alive."

"No," she said, agreeing. "Doesn't make sense."

"Unless there's some terrible secret that Brant knew about. Let's suppose that when Howard Holton went to the hotel to meet with Brant, Fiona went along. Or met him there, it doesn't really matter. The point is, Brant was killed and she ran away. And Margolis got caught in the middle. You know why I'm sure Fiona is involved? Because Margolis was old school, very cautious. Not likely he'd have turned his back on a man he suspected of murder. Either Fiona distracted him so that Holton could wack him from behind, or she was swinging the club herself. At the very least she's an accessory to murder. Or anyhow that's my current theory."

Meg stood up and tried to hook her thumbs in her jean pockets. Missed and thought missing was funny.

"You better sit down," I suggested. "You just polished off six ounces of eighty-proof in less than twenty minutes. It's gone to your head."

She came to me, being very careful not to trip over her feet, perched on my lap, and gave me a warm whiskey-scented kiss. I didn't mind. Booze or not, it felt real.

"Fuck it," she whispered. "Nan-*tuck*-et."

"What?" I said. "What about Nantucket?"

It was too late. She was already sound asleep.

26

Meg was still snoozing comfortably when I rolled into the bedroom and put her to bed. Crawling in beside her, I whispered her name once. No response. And no further explanation of the tantalizing *Fuck it, Nantucket* phrase that remained unfurled in my head.

As Megan normally swore only for effect, not from habit, I had to assume the phrase could be translated as *Oh, the hell with it, the big secret I've been keeping from you is Nantucket.*

Well, okay. But what *about* Nantucket? There were a number of possible connections.

1. Meg's mother lived on the island.
2. We'd recently been married there.
3. Howard Holton had drowned in the Nantucket surf.

Assuming that Meg wasn't intending to move back in with her mother or seeking to have our marriage annulled, I settled on the third option. The Holton connection.

As I drifted off, snuggled comfortably, I willed myself into a dream. It is a summer dream and I am on a beach with Howard Holton. The sand is warm under my feet. Howard is jogging through the surf, running to keep up with his fish. He holds the rod high, reeling as he runs. I run through the sand, trying to keep up. The sun blazes through a rising wave and makes it hard to see him clearly. In the blur of the dream I glimpse the beard that hides his face, the intensely sad blue eyes.

Go, H-Man! I cheer him on. Running in the sand alongside the crashing surf, my legs strong and light under me. Running and running. The wave keeps rising and I keep running.

It is a lovely, terrible dream.

We were on the road by eight. Meg, up at the crack of dawn, had cabbed into Cambridge, paid off the tow yard, and returned the van to Beacon Street with only a few minor tow-yard scratches.

"You're amazing," I told her as we edged into slow moving traffic on the Southeast Expressway. "Last night you passed out, this morning you're bright eyed and bushy tailed."

"I didn't 'pass out,' Jack. I wanted to cuddle but I didn't want to talk."

"Very convenient."

"You seemed to like it well enough."

Indeed. I felt whole again. The fear of apartness, of numbing distance, was again submerged.

In high summer the road south would have been a parking lot, but on a fine day in March we made good time, cutting across the shoulder of the Cape toward Buzzard's Bay. Megan in a quiet but responsive mood. Naming the island had not been a slip of the whiskey tongue, she had intended that we make the trip. It was, in every sense, her idea.

"I don't *know* that Fiona is there," she said, pouring coffee from a thermos as we made the last winding run into Woods Hole. "It's my best guess. Early on, before she went back to Lynda's, she mentioned the cottage as a place of refuge. Sort of wistful."

"So she's been there before?"

Meg nodded.

"And Howard," I said. "Will he be there, too?"

"I don't know," she said. "I really don't."

As we headed south into the coming season I decided not to push her on the subject. It was enough that she was beginning to share. Meg sipped her coffee, turned her face to the mild winter light. Spring comes early to the Cape and already there were buds on the trees, signs of the green that would soon awaken.

Woods Hole is a small, lovely town facing the Sound, with Buzzard's Bay tapping at the back door, so to speak. A place that thrives on sea and salt, home to the famous Oceanographic Institute and the island ferry service. That morning a light fog drifted in from the southeast, and it made the water black. The *Nantucket* was waiting, hull open, ready to swallow up motor vehicles, passengers, a few hardy bicyclists. Meg ran into the Steamship Authority office while I jockeyed for a place in line.

"You don't mind?" she said, returning with tickets.

"I'm getting used to it," I said.

Boats and I don't get along. Small, open-deck ferries have an oddly claustrophobic effect on me, but the *Nantucket* was big enough to have a sturdy, shiplike feel. The passage took several hours so there was no need to stay cooped up in the van. We found an accessible place on the lower deck—shipboard transitions in a wheelchair are a bitch because of the way the doorjambs are cut, leaving several inches of steel to negotiate. We settled in for the voyage or passage or trip or whatever the hell it is that old salts call getting from here to there.

"Did you take your Dramamine?"

"Yes, ma'am."

"You told me to remind you."

"Yes, and you just did. Thanks. I'll be fine."

On the way out for our Christmas Eve wedding,

the seas had been rough. Long, high-rolling swells that had come all the way from Spain to ruin my day. This time out the water was reassuringly flat and I vowed to make a sacrifice to Neptune or Exxon or whatever water god was calling the shots these days.

Meg occupied herself with the *New York Times* and the *Globe*. I made sure my wheels were locked just in case the smooth water was a ruse and then opened the bound galleys of *Fatal Knowledge*, the soon-to-be-published novel Howard H. Holton had finished just before the surf snatched him away. Fran Dixon, his editor, had sent it along with a short note asking that I not circulate the manuscript.

As usual Holton hooked me with the opening sentence: *It lay there in the gutter like a white thing the wind couldn't touch, neither dead nor alive.*

Not a bad way to describe a carnation that has just been discarded by a hit man as he enters a restaurant in Little Italy. And if you anticipate that the hit man is about to assassinate a Mafia don, you guessed wrong, because in a Howard H. Holton novel nothing ever proceeds according to formula.

Okay, I'll give you this much: The hit man goes into his favorite café, orders his favorite drink, drinks it, produces a gun, and demands that the other patrons leave at once. Get a mop and a bucket, he tells the terrified bartender. And while the bartender is fetching the mop, the hit man shoots himself in the heart.

All in three terse, compelling, Holtonesque pages.

"How is it?" Meg asked me about an hour out of Woods Hole.

"Maybe his best," I said. "If he doesn't blow the ending."

He didn't. I finished the final chapter as the ferry rounded up into the channel. The fog had lifted and the village of Nantucket was bright in the sunlight.

"Son of a bitch," I said, tossing the galleys into Megan's carryall. "I can't believe it. He killed him off."

"What?"

"Holton killed off his main character. He's ended the series."

Meg gave me a look. "Let me guess. A woman kills him, right?"

I hesitated.

"I knew it," she said.

"The strange thing is, he *deserved* to die," I said. "And before you say it's typical, misogynistic Howard H. Holton, the woman who kills off the detective is a nurse, disconnecting him from life support. She believes she's doing the right thing. And, damn it, Holton made me *agree* with her."

Passengers were heading for their vehicles as the ferry homed in on the wharf slot, slipping between the pilings and the giant bumpers.

"Remember what they say about death," Meg said, slinging the carryall up on her shoulder.

"So," I said, waiting, "what *do* they say?"

"It is but a transition."

The cottage was in Madaket, near the western tip of the island. Meg, who knew the way, directed me through the narrow streets of Nantucket proper—and proper it is, with mandatory white slat fences and just-so weathered shingles that keep the local carpenters busy. No longer an island of fishermen, Nantucket has become a tourist destination, a showplace for the wealthy off-islanders who have bought and restored so many of the native homes.

Off-islanders like Howard H. Holton. I didn't even want to venture a guess as to the cost of a waterfront cottage, but Holton had been justly proud of acquiring it on his book earnings. He'd joined a long line of writers who had made a seasonal home there, from Melville through the Benchleys, although it had not yet—thankfully—become a celebrity destination on the order of the nearby Vineyard.

The winding road to Madaket traversed grassy dunes, a landscape at once barren and beautiful, with glimpses of the fog-grayed, shore-gnawing Atlantic. Meg had a pensive look as she searched through her purse.

"Pull over here," she said, indicating an unpaved road.

"This goes down to the beach?"

She nodded. "What just a minute, though. I think you should look at this."

She handed me an empty pill bottle. A prescription for Ms. Fiona Darling. I read Fomalyn on the label and shrugged. "So?"

"So I found it in the bathroom. That night at the loft. Remember you suggested I check the medicine cabinet, see if she'd really left?"

"Vaguely."

"I looked it up. Fomalyn is a brand of female hormone."

"But why. . ." I began, and then stopped. The idea took my breath away. And yet there it was, an explanation so simple but so utterly foreign to my way of thinking that it hadn't occurred.

Meg smiled, patted my hand.

"I had an inkling but it didn't really click until I saw that prescription. It was almost like she left it for me to find. Or for *someone* to find."

I shuddered, shook my head.

Arthur Conan Doyle said it best. When you have eliminated the impossible, whatever remains, however improbable, must be the truth. And yet this "truth" that Meg had sprung on me was so strange and alien it begged denial. "It's only an empty pill bottle," I said, aware of a pleading in my voice. "There has to be some other explanation."

"That's what we're here to find out," Meg said. "Drive on. Let's get this over with."

The unpaved road twisted through a terrain of grassy dunes and scrub pines pushing up through the sandy soil. Rabbit country. I kept the speed low because the furry little buggers seemed to make a game of it, leaping out at the last possible instant.

The road dead-ended where three similar gray-shingled cottages overlooked an eroded bluff. Two of the buildings were battened down for the season. The third had shutters open. A thin plume of smoke rose from a beachstone chimney. There was a familiar, decrepit Volkswagen Beetle beside the cottage, tires buried up to the hubs in the sand.

"How shall we do this?" I said.

"We don't want to be sneaky."

"Heavens, no," I said.

"I mean we want to gain her trust again, right? If you're interested in the truth."

"Oh, I am," I said, and parked in such a way as to block the Volkswagen. "Seeker of truth, justice, and the American way, that's me."

"You think she'll try to run again?" Meg said.

"Not unless she can walk on the water."

I was slogging my way along the creaky planks that lead to the cottage when she appeared on the porch, wrapped in a shawl. The wind came off the sea, shivering the beach grass, making the sand crawl.

"I've been expecting you," she said, holding herself rigid.

I said, "Hello, Howard. Or do you prefer H-man?"

"Call me Fiona," she said. "Please?"

27

Driftwood makes a pretty fire. The sea salts glow in the heat, giving up soft colors and a sigh of bright sparks. Fiona carefully settled more wood into the flames, keeping her back to me as she spoke.

"You'll want lunch. Are sandwiches okay?"

"Fiona, we have to talk."

"Yes, of course. But lunch first. I've made some bread, it's just cooling now."

While I positioned my chair close by the fire, Megan prowled the cottage. It was typical beach-style, one large room divided up by partition walls of knotty pine into two small bedrooms, a working/living area, and a small kitchen in the back. Surrounding porches would, in season, double the living space and provide somewhat sheltered sleeping quarters for warm-weather guests. There were books everywhere, on shelves, in stacks, underfoot. Holton's fishing gear was stored above the exposed rafters; sturdy surf-casting rods, waders, gaffs. Fiona's word processor had been set up on a worktable by a window that faced the sea. File folders were neatly stacked beside the keyboard, along with a pad of lined, legal-size paper and a Smuckers jam jar full of sharpened yellow pencils.

"My God," Meg said, staring out the window at the ripple-line of waves. "What a beautiful place this is."

From behind the kitchen partition, Fiona spoke. "I'm getting a lot of work done. I'd never been here alone before, or at this time of year. No phone, no neighbors, no one on the beach. It's different."

We ate by the fire, off souvenir trays that depicted

views of the island. Albacore tuna, homemade bread, and garlic dills on the side. Fiona carried in mugs of strong, hot tea sweetened with honey.

"The bread is yummy," Megan said. She'd settled herself into a rocker next to me. The two of us facing Fiona, who occupied an old, unpainted wicker chair.

"Thanks," Fiona said. "Jack, you're not eating."

"My stomach's a bit unsettled."

"Oh?"

"The ferry. I took a pill."

"Would you prefer soup? All I've got is the canned stuff."

"I'm fine. Fiona. And the bread really does smell delicious."

She nodded, fiddled with the food on her plate. Studying her complexion now, in light of what I knew, I could discern the faint pockmarks and electrolysis scars under the layer of makeup.

She said, "I've established a routine. I get up at dawn, put on my face, and start the dough. Then I do a beach patrol, for the driftwood. That's an adventure. You wouldn't believe the stuff that fetches up on this shore. Yesterday I found this crate? You know what was in it? Light bulbs. From Yugoslavia, of all places. Isn't that amazing?"

We agreed that it was amazing.

"When I've got enough wood for the day I put the bread in the oven, set the timer, and get to work."

"Sounds very homey," Meg said.

"It is. I'm happy here."

"Guess what happened to Jack, Fiona?" Meg said with an edge to her voice. "He got arrested, trying to find you."

"Oh?"

Meg recounted my adventures as a night burglar. She made it sound almost amusing. Maybe I would feel that way about it, too, given time. Right now I was still struggling with the incredible transformation of Howard H. Holton, two-fisted crime writer and womanizer, into the seemingly gentle, ascetically inclined Fiona Darling.

"I'm sorry for all the trouble," Fiona said. "You understand, as soon as I found Brant dead in that damn hotel I knew it was over. I couldn't be a secret anymore. But I just wasn't ready. I didn't know how to do it. I still don't."

"How to do what?"

"Come back to life," she said. "Become a freak."

This was spoken matter-of-factly, without bitterness. She might have been remarking on a spot of bad weather. As Fiona shifted in her seat and looked full at me for the first time, I realized with a start that her eyes were now blue.

Howard Holton's eyes staring out of a woman's face.

"Contacts," she said with a slight smile. "They've been bothering me lately, so I stopped wearing them. Why bother changing my eye color when there's no one to see the difference?"

"I never suspected," I said. "But then I never met Howard in person—the beard hid most of his face, come to think of it."

"Yes," she said. "Howard was always hiding."

"Tell me this, Fiona. You wanted to change your sex, right? That's fairly rare but no longer unique or illegal. Why did you fake your death? Why stage the drowning?"

"Do we have to talk about this?"

"Yes," I said. "Brant Sturne is dead. Ted Margolis is dead. Yes, we have to talk about this."

"You don't think I had anything to do with poor Brant or the investigator?"

"Convince us," I said.

Fiona sighed, put aside the lunch tray. Apparerntly her appetite was no stronger than mine. "You have to understand how much I hated him," she said. "Howard H. Holton, the phony, the fake. Every day of that man's life was a lie."

She seemed determined to talk about her former self in the third person. I found myself falling into the same rhythm. "Was Howard really an alcoholic?" I asked. "Or was that a cover story?"

"Cover story?" Fiona shook her head, fixed a prim, schoolmarmish smile. "That was one thing about Howard that was real enough. He was a bad drunk. They say there are as many reasons to drink as there are drunks, but Howard drank to get away from Howard and of course *that* never worked. As the years went by he found himself addicted. He had to give it up before he made the change."

"So your, um, change was planned well ahead of time?"

Fiona laughed at the way I stumbled around the word. "Of course it was planned. Do you suppose that transsexual surgery is available at the local clinic? Or that you can *have* one, just like that?"

"I never gave it a lot of thought," I said.

"Why would you? You're at home in your own body, your own gender. I'll bet when you close your eyes, in your secret heart you're still a little boy. The child inside every adult."

"I suppose I am."

"Well, I was always a little girl. That's how I pictured myself from the very beginning. I was about five years old before I realized other little boys didn't think of themselves as little girls. I got in a fight over it, as a matter of fact, and that started the pattern."

"What pattern, Fiona?"

"The pattern of self-destruction. Of hating my own body. Because, you see, it wasn't the *right* body. A mistake had been made. A terrible mistake."

"You knew this when you were five?"

"I always knew it. I have very vivid memories of my early childhood. I distinctly remember being three years old. I know exactly what my bedroom looked like, how it felt to be that small, what I thought about when I was alone. I remember what it was like *under* the bed, because I used to hide there. A lot."

Meg said, "You were an abused child?"

Fiona shook her head. "Oh no. Not at all. My parents adored me. Whatever was wrong with me, it had nothing to do with abuse or trauma. It was inside me from the minute I was born—probably from my moment of conception." She paused, used a stick to poke the fire. A swarm of sparks detached themselves from the flames and fled upwards. "There are all sorts of theories about how a child develops cross-gender identification, but no scientific proof. I tend to think it's genetic, at least it was with me. I was a girl baby born with a serious birth defect—a male body."

"And you kept these feelings secret?" Meg asked.

"Oh yes. Oh my, yes. You learn fast when you're a freak. You learn to hide what makes you different, what keeps you apart. That fight I mentioned, when I was five years old? That was the first time I ever told my true feelings to anyone—and the last. Until Dr. Foster finally got me to open up. Thirty-five years of denial. But you already know that if you read her notes."

"I never saw the notes," I said. "She'd taken them out of the files."

"Good for Helen, she's fiercely protective of her patients. Her 'clients,' that's the word they prefer now. But I was very much a patient, a sick person in need of healing. And Dr. Foster helped the healing start."

"She knew that Howard Holton was going to fake his own death?"

Fiona shook her head vigorously. "No. Absolutely not. And after it happened she strongly disapproved. She wanted me to make the change openly, to find a way to live with the consequences. But that would have meant facing Tasha and Brant and an entire world of people who knew only Howard Holton. I simply couldn't face it."

"So you drowned."

Fiona got up, went to the window facing the sea. Megan and I let her have her silence.

"It was so easy," she said. "All I did was buy a used car. Five hundred bucks, that's what it took to make Howard Holton vanish."

"I don't get it. What does a car have to do with it?"

Fiona smiled. "Everything, Jack. The car was my escape vehicle. I parked that little old Volkswagen on a dead-end road about a half-mile down the beach. I had it in mind I wouldn't go ahead with it until I actually had a fish on the line. Last chance for H-Man to do his thing, see? We came up here on a Friday, a whole crowd of us, and it wasn't until Sunday that I finally managed to hook up. Two solid days of throwing that damn lure into the surf. Of course I had a reputation to keep up. Howard Holton, outdoorsman, so fired up about landing a silly bluefish that he gets himself drowned."

"You what, swam away?"

She turned from the window, crossed her arms over her bosom. "It was easier than it sounds. The way the bluff runs here, and the dunes, you can't really see that much of the shoreline from the porch. All I had to do was get around the corner, then crawl up into the dunes. I walked to the Volkswagen, shaved off my beard, and took the next ferry back to the mainland. Stayed belowdecks in the car the whole trip, just on the off chance there was anybody who might have recognized me even with my beard off."

"You make it sound so simple."

"It *was* simple. The best plots are dead simple, you know that Jack."

The author-ego in me wondered if he'd read any of my books, but something in me didn't really want to know. "This wasn't a book, Fiona," I said. "You left a world behind. A world full of people. Some of whom cared a lot for Howard Holton."

We hit another patch of silence then, as Fiona studied the waves. By now I knew not to prod her. Or the him that still remained hidden inside of her.

"It was like this," she said at last. "Either I faked Howard's death or I really and truly killed myself. That was my choice. And for better or worse I chose that Howard should die so I could live."

A storm blew in soon after lunch. You could feel the wind pressing against the cottage walls, whistling down the beach grass, singing tunelessly in the chimney. The seas flattened when the squall hit, driving long, shimmering knife cuts of rain. The water drummed violently against the windows, then stopped as abruptly as it had begun.

"We're on the edge of the Gulf Stream here," Fiona said. "It makes for strange weather patterns. Two summers ago there was hail as big as golfballs—the fish wouldn't bite for days after."

"Maybe they were playing underwater golf."

"Maybe," Fiona said. "Anything is possible, right?"

"Anything."

We talked, off and on, for most of the afternoon. It was as if Meg and I were stand-ins for Dr. Foster. The conversation—more a soliloquy, really—was some-times disjointed, jumping around in time, at other times powerfully focused, with the crisp rhetoric of the old Howard Holton somehow mixed up with the insightful observations of the new Fiona Darling.

"I can't explain the physical attraction thing," she said. "All I can tell you is that wanting to be a woman didn't prevent me from being *attracted* to certain women. Tasha and I were hot for each other, at least in the beginning. In the early years. What she never knew is that I found her attractive because I wanted to be *like* her. Most of the time I didn't think about it myself, I just reacted. And of course the booze made it worse. The booze distorted the distortion, does that make any sense?"

Meg and I made murmurs of agreement. Although I couldn't identify or even fully comprehend the demons that had tormented Howard Holton, and continued to haunt Fiona Darling, I knew what it meant to feel a freak. That much I knew.

"I know now how wrong it was of me to marry Tasha," he said. "Not that we didn't love each other. But love isn't enough. I needed that *closeness* I could never have. More than sex, I wanted intimacy, can you understand that?"

Megan glanced at me. The glance itself was loaded with the very intimacy and closeness Fiona described with such longing. That, too, was a need I could easily comprehend.

"Is it any better now?" I asked, somewhat indelicately.

Fiona looked away. "Not the intimacy, no. But I've given up on wanting that. I don't see myself sharing this life with anyone. Who would want it? No, I'll just have to settle for being able to look in the mirror and see my real self."

"More than your gender has changed," I said. "I read *Sea Change*. It's a new voice. There are similarities to Holton, of course—the way you use the language—but the personality behind the words is different."

"It's not really a conscious change," she said. "I just find myself interested in different things. And so I write about different things."

"But still crime and human frailties."

"Yes. The theme is the same—but a new voice is singing."

"No regrets?" I said.

"I have many regrets," she said. "But not about the operation. The transition, if you will. It's almost like I've *molted*, you know? Gotten rid of this old, ugly skin that was choking the life out of me."

"Howard was that bad?"

"For me he was. Some transsexuals enter into gay relationships, or become weekend transvestites to ease the pain. Howard did the other thing, he went total macho, made himself act the part of the conquering male who treats women as plunder. That's the only way he knew how to respond."

"It was there in the books," I said. "That tension. I never thought of it as sexual, though."

"It was more than that," Fiona said. "Howard saw violence and risk-taking as an essential masculine attribute, and so he wrote about violence and risk. The whole Hemingway mystique. The creative tough guy, always testing himself, in love with the idea that self-creation is linked to self-destruction." She paused, smiled warily. "It sounds like psycho-babble, I know, but the truth is imbedded in the jargon."

"What about the truth of Brant Sturne," I said. "He seemed very devoted to Howard Holton."

Fiona's eyes filled with tears. "Poor Brant. He was

even more tormented than I was—than Howard was. When I paired up with Tasha, Brant was still a little boy. He wanted a father, a mother, a big brother, he wanted *somebody* to share with. Howard did his best. He could see quite a lot of himself in Brant. Brant was part of Tasha's attraction, a way for Howard to reach back into his childhood and set things right."

"And *did* you set things right?"

Fiona shook her head sadly. "You know I didn't, Jack. The adult Brant was a mess. More miserable than the adult Howard, if such a thing is possible. Howard equated sex with domination—Brant equated it with death, with the act of dying."

"Brant wasn't a suicide, Fiona. He was murdered."

"I know that now, of course. But when I saw him hanging from that chandelier I thought he'd killed himself to punish me. And so I ran away. I didn't really stop until I got here, to this place."

"And you have no idea who killed him?"

"None."

I said, "Until just a few hours ago my favorite suspect was Howard Holton."

"Howard no longer exists, Jack. He was surgically extinguished. And for all his faults, he wasn't a killer."

"But how did Brant know about Fiona?"

She shrugged, stirred the glowing coals in the fireplace. "He was a very intuitive boy. From what I gather he never believed that Howard had really drowned and so he hired Fitzroy Security to track me down."

"I thought Tasha hired them."

Fiona shook her head. "It was Brant. The Fitzroy investigator found Howard's name was on the deed to the loft and then discovered I was living there. I suppose he thought I was Howard's mistress, the reason he'd been coming up to Boston every week."

"You mean it was Brant who read *Sea Change*? Cooked up a lawsuit?"

"Yes. He persuaded Tasha to bring the lawyers in. Thought if they created enough trouble for Fiona, Howard would have to step forward."

"Brant told you all this?"

"Most of it," she said. "What happened is that one night the phone rang and I picked it up and said hello and Brant recognized my voice."

Fiona explained that her speaking voice was the one thing that hadn't changed all that much. Although slightly altered in pitch by the hormone treatment, it was still recognizable.

"When did this happen?" Meg asked. "When did he call?"

"Right after you two came back from New York. Whatever you said to him about Fiona, it made him more suspicious than ever. So he decided to confront her directly."

"And you told him the truth?"

Fiona hesitated, shook her head. "No. He sounded so happy to know that Howard was alive, I just couldn't. And I thought, well, Tasha would never accept the new me, but Brant might. Maybe I owed him that much, to give it a try. In any case I agreed to meet with him if he came to Boston. Alone."

"And was he alone?" I said.

"I don't know. All I know is that he called me shortly after he checked into the hotel—and when I got there he was dead."

"Did you know that Margolis was tailing you that night?"

"No. Do *you* know that he was? I've been thinking about that a lot. Maybe what happened is that Brant was planning a party."

"A party?" Megan asked.

Fiona nodded. "It would have been just like him. Making a game of it. Invite all his friends. You two and also the Fitzroy investigator. Make Howard the surprise guest."

"So Margolis shows up on cue, discovers Brant dead. But why wouldn't he notify the police? Why go chasing out to the warehouse?"

"All I have is a theory," Fiona said.

"Let's hear it."

"Assume he followed the killer," she said. "And the killer led him to my place. Maybe the killer was looking for me. Don't ask me why—I still have no idea why anyone would want Brant dead."

Meg said, "You think that whoever killed Brant wants to kill you?"

"I'm saying it's a possibility. A theory."

"What about a motive?" Meg said.

Fiona chuckled. "Just like an editor," she said. "Wants to keep the plot tight. Make sure every crime has a motive. Maybe this crime doesn't *have* a motive, Megan. Maybe the killer just likes to kill."

I interrupted. "Hang on. There *is* a possible motive. Suppose the killer thought you saw him in Brant's room, or even near it. He'd want to elimate a witness."

"But I didn't see anyone."

"Think about it. You must have seen *someone*. It's a great big, busy hotel."

Fiona waved it off. "Nobody I recognized. Nobody I knew."

"But how could a killer *know* that? Or be sure you wouldn't be able to pull him out of a lineup later?"

"He couldn't," Fiona conceded. "Okay, so we have another theory to consider. But we still don't know why Brant was killed. Or by whom."

"No," I said. "But we do know one thing. Once the police discover that you and Howard Holton are the same person . . ."

Fiona interrupted, "But we're not!"

"Excuse me, but the Homicide boys may not bother with the fine distinctions. They're not likely to see the need for a mysterious, unidentified killer who follows you from the hotel, and who in turn is followed by Ted Margolis. They'll be inclined to keep it nice and simple. Brant discovered your secret and threatened to spill the beans and so you killed him. And Margolis confronted you with the evidence and so you killed him, too."

"But I didn't."

"Maybe not."

"I *didn't.*"

"Okay. But what Meg and I take on faith, the cops will only take on proof."

Fiona gave me a look. "Whatever happened to innocent until proven guilty?"

I said, "That only happens in books."

28

egan's mother was in Florida visiting relatives, so we had the Drew residence all to ourselves. It was a cozy, comfortable cape not far from the old windmill, convenient to the center of town without being right in the middle of things. In season the roof trellis was a blaze of red roses, which had got it featured on an island postcard. There were two bedrooms upstairs, but my sensible, kind-hearted mother-in-law had installed a convertible couch in what she called the drawing room, so that I wouldn't have to fight the stairs when visiting.

"I need a long hot shower," Meg announced right off.

She put her carryall down, ducked into the downstairs bath. A few moments later, naked and lovely, she came back out to get a fresh towel and said, "Are you going to call Larry Sheehan? Or Russ White?"

"Maybe," I said.

"She's vulnerable as hell," Meg reminded me. "Headlines won't help."

A moment later the water came on. Have I mentioned that Megan Drew whistles in the shower? Those who consider shower whistling a strictly male activity haven't heard Meg in action. The effect is stimulating to the ear, and elsewhere. I offered to scrub her back, did so, and what with one thing and another the sun was well down before we returned to the subject of what to do about Fiona Darling.

"You know what he's done, don't you?" I said, propping myself up on the pillows.

"You mean the operation?" Meg was lying with her

head on my chest. Her voice made a vibration that tickled my flesh.

"More than the operation. That was a physical change. The real miracle is that he's created Fiona Darling," I said, rising to the subject. "Talk about making your characters come to life! My God, Megan, he's taken a fictional creation and endowed her with actual physical attributes!"

Meg gave me a strange look. "You sound almost jealous."

"Come on," I said, stirring uncomfortably. "You don't think that, do you?"

She laughed. "The look on your face, Jack. You were imagining being castrated, right?"

I nodded. "My instincts recoil—not even for literary immortality would I submit to that. But you have to admire the nerve. For having the courage of his or her convictions."

"Make it her. You believed she was a real woman and so did I. She obviously believes it."

"That makes it true?"

Relinquishing her place on my chest, Meg sat up and punched a pillow into shape. "What *is* the truth, Jack? Fiona has been surgically altered, she's on hormone therapy. She lives, breathes, thinks, and acts like a woman." Meg paused, leaned forward to whisper. "She sits down to pee, Jack. Very important distinction there. A brave new world of toilet seats."

That struck me as funny. Or possibly it was nerves that made me laugh. "Surgically altered, yes, but it's really cosmetic. She doesn't have a womb," I pointed out. "She can't have babies."

Megan scowled. I'd made her angry.

"So?" she said. "Does that mean a woman who's had a hysterectomy is no longer a woman?"

"I, ah, hadn't thought of it that way."

"Fiona is not a freak," Meg said. "She's a living breathing human being."

"Of course. That's what I was getting at," I said, somewhat lamely.

Meg softened, but my gut reaction about a womb defining womanhood was out there, naked, with no way for me to take it back. I should have known better—nothing makes me so angry as those ignorant few who assume a wheelchair means a loss of manhood. Of all people, I knew that gender isn't defined by physical equipment, or the lack of it.

I frowned, reached to caress Meg. She did not resist.

"It's not something I have to think about a lot," I said. "Not since you came into my life."

Megan kissed me. Her cheeks were moist.

"That poor woman, all alone in that beautiful place and no one to share her life. You know how lucky we are?"

"Yes," I said, and meant it.

We napped for a while and woke up famished. Megan threw on some clothes—she's a much faster dresser than I, for obvious reasons—and went into her mother's kitchen.

A minute later she was back to report.

"Nothing in the fridge, Mr. Hawkins. Whatever shall we do?"

We decided to try a new restaurant not far from the ferry dock and the bike rental shops. Queequeg's Chowder House. It sounded touristy but served a mean and not too lean bowl of soup. Pardon me, chowder. Your choice of styles, New York or New England, with locally harvested bay scallops substituting for clams.

I went the New York route, strictly out of perversity, while Megan stayed loyal to the area.

"Tomatoes in chowder make it not-chowder," she insisted.

"Delicious, this not-chowder. And slightly mysterious."

"How so?"

"Queequeg was rumored to be a cannibal," I said. "What do you suppose is the secret ingredient here?"

She tasted from my bowl. "A little thyme," she said. "A little dried basil. Notice how we're not talking about Fiona?"

"I hadn't," I said. "Now, obviously, we are."

Megan buttered a chowder cracker. "Decision time, Jack. Fiona is wanted for questioning in two murders. We know where she is. What do we do?"

"Finish our supper, have a drink, think about it?"

That seemed reasonable. We adjourned to the lounge, found a table that was not bombarded by big-screen microwave pulses—the Bruins (pronounced "Broons") were skating on thin ice to the enthusiastic approval of the bar-thumping patrons—and proceeded to think about it.

Thinking about Fiona was hard and thirsty work.

"You know what I keep thinking?" I said after the third beer. "I keep thinking, would Tommy the bartender want to know? Or would he prefer the Howard Holton he remembers?"

"It's not up to Tommy, or any of Howard's old friends."

"No."

"It should be up to Fiona."

A ragged cheer from the bar as the Broons scored again. The team was having a good season, the best since the Bobby Orr years, and it was hoped they wouldn't ruin a longstanding Boston sports tradition by winning it all.

"I know you believe that," I said. "And I respect your opinion. Loyalty is one of the many things I love about you, Megan."

"But you disagree."

"Inclining that way. Howard Holton didn't live alone in the world. When he faked his death he uttered a lie that is still resonating. Two people are dead. Not to mention that you lost your job."

"I don't care about that. The job part."

"Yes, you do. You had the sense to recognize talent when you saw it and you were punished for doing good work. It has to hurt. Your outlook has changed—you'll never think of publishing in quite the same way. Because of Fiona."

"That wasn't *her* fault. And neither was Brant."

"You're sure about that?"

"Whatever else she may or may not be, Fiona Darling is not a killer."

"I think Brant died because Howard lied about his own death."

"How do you know that?"

"The same way you know Fiona isn't capable of murder. Instinct. Something in my guts. I know it because lies kill people. Lies are a cancer, they eat up society, they devour human decency. Bad things happen when people lie, even when *good* people lie."

Megan folded her arms. I was aware of how pompous my mini-lecture sounded. What did I, a novelist, a *fictionalizer* of human behavior, know about the truth?

"You're right about lies," Meg said, "except you've got it backward. Howard Holton was the lie. Fiona Darling is the truth."

Women. They stick together, even when some of them used to be men.

29

Morning in Nantucket. The plan was to take the second ferry back, allowing time to digest a light breakfast before embarking on a nauseating, medicated sea voyage. The decision about sharing or not sharing our knowledge of what had happened to Howard H. Holton could wait until we were on home turf, in possession of such facts as might still be arising.

"When in doubt, delay, is that it?"

"Absolutely," I said. "*Mañana* is one of the most beautiful words in any language."

I should have realized that it doesn't always matter if you're looking back, or choosing not to look forward. Things catch up.

What happened is that I decided to dial our Boston number and monitor the messages left on our answering machine. Fitzy was supposed to get back to me about my upcoming court date—I still had a felony charge to beat, and I was hoping that Dr. Helen Foster might change her mind once she'd had a chance to cool off.

Fitzy hadn't left a message. Most of the tape was taken up by Russ White, who had called several times and been recorded in various stages of urgency.

Russ here. Hey Jack, are you related to the Hawkins just got himself busted on a Cambridge break-in? And if not, how come nobody is home to answer the phone? Riddle me that, Hawk man.

followed by

Russ again. Call me at work.

and

Russ White, kid reporter. Are you there, Hawkins? Are you one of those creeps who screen calls?
and finally
Things are breaking here, Jack. Do you want to be part of it or not?

When I looked up from the phone Meg was studying me.

"Russ sounds excited about something," I explained. "I better call him."

"Ferry leaves in half an hour," she pointed out.

"Won't take a minute," I said, dialing his work number. The minute stretched into several more—Mr. White wasn't at his desk but was rumored to be in the vicinity.

"Jack, we really need to get in line."

Right about then Russ came to the phone: "Hawkins! Where have you been? We got the big break, thanks to Mary Beth. She managed to ferret out the real owner of Hub City Realty Trust."

"Hub City who?" I said.

Meg was pointing at her watch and silently mouthing *missing the boat.*

"Hub City Realty Trust controls the option on the parking garage facility. The Sturne Royal Hotel? The lack of parking? The thirteen-million pricetag? Is this ringing any bells, Jack?"

"Tell me who," I said.

Russ named the name. Bells were ringing then, loud and clear.

"Have you told Detective Sheehan?"

"Sure, of course. Right after I called you the first time."

"Is he going to make an arrest?" I asked.

Megan froze on the word "arrest," then put down her carryall and came closer to the phone.

"Sheehan says it's too soon for an arrest," Russ

was saying. "He's over there now, the hotel, interviewing the staff, see if he can place the suspect at the scene the night Brant Sturne was murdered."

"Russ? Great work. Give Mary Beth a hug or a kiss or whatever you can afford. But there's more happening here than just the money angle."

"Yeah? Tell me about it, for chrissake."

"Later, Russ."

I hung up, stared out the window at the innocent blue sky, and shook my head.

"Speak," Meg insisted.

"Tasha's lawyer," I said. "Thurston Breen, Jr. He stands to make umpteen millions if Sturne International buys the parking garage."

I didn't regret missing the ferry. Any excuse to put off having my horizons altered. Instead we turned left at the bottom of the street and took the road to Madaket.

"There's something we should keep in mind," I said. "Just because young Thurston is in line for the loot, it doesn't necessarily mean he killed Brant. Or for that matter Ted Margolis."

"Fiona will know," Meg said with confidence.

She had her arms crossed tight against her breasts, knees together, feet up on the dash. Megan Drew, tense and guarded; I knew the posture.

"That smug bastard," she said. "Never trust a man with two last names."

Spring had smuggled itself into the island sometime during the night. There was a softness in the air, a sense of green things about to happen. Birds darted through the dune grasses, showing off bits of sudden color, tumbling up into the sky. Season of change and hope—and sometimes of a hunger so rapacious that the weak cannot survive.

"Fiona is going to have to take a stand," I said, turning into the dead-end road. "Maybe *the* stand. Do you think she's strong enough for that? Facing the world in court?"

"Not for me to say."

All the way out to Madaket I'd worried that the battered Volkswagen would not be there, that we'd find the cottage shut up. Not to worry, the Bug had not moved and the little chimney exuded a stream of white smoke. The surprise was a brand-new sedan parked in such a way as to block the road.

"That's an airport rental," Meg said, squinting at the sticker on the bumper.

There was a seasick feeling in my belly as the lift dropped me to the sand. Dry land or not I felt in need of a Dramamine. And I almost jumped out of my chair when the kitchen door opened with a sound like a gunshot.

"I'll be darned," Thurston Breen, Jr., said. "Look what the cat dragged in."

30

From inside came the sound of a woman sobbing. Megan went in ahead while I allowed Thurston to assist in getting the chair up the porch steps. I could feel his breath on the top of my head as he pulled from behind.

"Tasha's in shock," he said. "Can't say I blame her."

"Been here long?" I said, swinging my chair around to face the inner door.

"Long enough," he said, keeping behind me. "I'd never have recognized him, but Tasha knew right away. Those blue eyes."

Inside I was greeted by a tableau of beautiful, angry despair. Fiona frozen in the wicker chair, staring into the flames. Tasha leaning against the mantel, face set like stone, her eyes as red as the coals in the fire. Megan caught between them, like an L Street Brownie gathering the courage to wade into Dorchester Bay on the coldest day in January. Scattered on the floor were pages from a manuscript, a life thrown down in anger.

Fiona looked up, found my eyes, and said, "I wish you hadn't."

"It wasn't me," I said. "We haven't told anyone yet."

"Not your fault, I suppose, but you were tailed."

"We didn't know," Meg said.

"You're not supposed to," Fiona sighed.

"Fitzroy Security put you both under surveillance after their investigator was killed," said Thurston.

He had moved to the fireplace, reaching out a consoling hand to Tasha. She shrank away. He shrugged, then flashed a calculated glance at me.

"Tasha agreed to pay the agency so long as they kept us informed of your whereabouts—the theory was that Fiona Darling would try to keep in contact with her editor. Locate Miss Darling and we might find Howard, if he was still alive." Thurston paused, shook his head ruefully. "Little did we know how true *that* was . . ."

"Why did you do this to me?" Tasha said, staring at Fiona. "How could you?"

Fiona was silent. She had the look of an animal frozen in the headlights of a speeding car. Doomed by the light but unable to run.

Tasha seemed to notice me for the first time. Her eyes were not friendly. "Is this some kind of horrible joke?" she said. "A game you writers play?"

"Nobody's laughing, Mrs. Holton."

Tasha started to say something, changed her mind and lurched to the couch. She pawed around inside her bulky, fashionable purse—larger than most backpacks—and came up with a crumpled pack of cigarettes. "I need a smoke," she announced. "I need a drink. I need to wake up from this sick, sick nightmare."

Thurston produced a lighter, clicking a flame into life. Tasha inhaled like a diver sucking oxygen through a kinked air hose. "Sorry about the drink," he said in a soothing, lawyer-to-client tone, "but Howard's on the wagon. Probably flushed all the booze away as soon as he got here. Right Howard?"

Fiona shuddered, then finally spoke in a clenched voice. "Bottle under the sink," she said. "My escape hatch."

Megan went into the kitchen, announced the discovery of a sealed fifth of vodka, and was instructed to pour Tasha a glass with two ice cubes. There were no other takers.

Tasha's smile was a terrible thing to behold as she raised the glass. "Here's to Howard's balls," she said. "Wherever they are."

Megan lowered herself into the rocking chair and gave me a look of inquiry. What were we to do? I shrugged, indicating that we had to let the confrontation play itself out.

The wound had been opened, now it had to bleed clean.

"You were never to know," Fiona said.

You had to strain to hear her.

"A divorce," Tasha said. "Normal people get divorced."

"He's not normal," Thurston said. He'd settled down next to his client, his legs comfortably crossed. He wore white twill trousers, a crewneck sweater, and weathered Topsider deck shoes without any socks. Preppy costuming for the islands. Not a care in the world. "You're not normal, are you, Howard?"

"Howard is dead. I'm Fiona."

The lawyer rolled his eyes. "Right. I forgot."

Tasha alternated greedy gulps at the vodka and the cigarette.

"What's your interest here, Hawkins?" Thurston said. "You keep popping up, I'm not sure why."

"Pending lawsuit," I said. "How soon you forget."

He nodded, as if he had indeed forgotten the lawsuit. "No problem," he said. "Consider it dropped."

"What?" Tasha said, her voice thickening. The sudden infusion of vodka was exacerbating her confusion and anger.

"Can't sue a man for stealing his own book, can we?"

"Oh, *book*," she said, making it a vile, four-letter word. "Howard and his *books*. Howie the hairy he-man novelist." The last was in a kind of cruel sing-song. She sucked the cigarette down to the filter, then flicked it into the fireplace. "'The Park Avenue Hemingway,' I think somebody called him. Except of course he didn't *live* on Park Avenue. But I guess 'Central Park South Hemingway' doesn't quite work. And anyhow old Hem didn't write crummy little mysteries, did he?" "Mysteries" came out "mishteries"—vodka on an empty stomach can hit like a jolt of heroin. "Ol' Hemingway, he never put on a dress, did he?" she said. "Never changed himself into a girl."

Fiona held herself still. The stillness of a crippled bird on a stormy shore, waiting for the wave to break.

"Hemingway had his own problems," I pointed out. "They took his booze away and he blew his brains out."

"Who ask you?" Tasha said. Her eyes had filmed over and I had the impression she didn't really remember who I was.

"The point is, we all have our demons," I said. "Hemingway was a suicide. Howard Holton found another way out."

Fiona gave a slight nod of agreement.

"That's shit, is what *that* is," Tasha said. "You writers, you're all full of shit."

So she did remember who I was.

"Fakers and liars." She leaned forward, stared at Fiona's bosom. "For instance those tits on your chest, Howard. Are they real? Huh?"

Fiona looked down at the floor. I had the impression she'd stopped breathing.

"Not that they're too big or too small or anything," Tasha said. "Just the right size, matter of fact. Very tasteful on a man your age. 'Scuze me, a *woman*."

Tasha didn't like writers or books but she certainly had a way with words. She made *woman* sound like *vermin*. Megan winced and I felt a little squirmy myself. Only the lawyer was at ease, casually adjusting the crease of his crisp white trousers. He was so obviously unconcerned—amused even—by the discovery that Howard Holton was alive, if transformed, that I began to wonder if Mary Beth Maxam's information was correct.

Could there be another Thurston Breen, Jr., involved in the real estate deal? Did the laws of coincidence stretch that far?

"Tasha, listen to me," Fiona said, her voice getting stronger. "I never meant to hurt you."

"You *hate* me."

"No," Fiona said. "I hated myself."

"You wanted me to think you were dead."

Fiona sighed. "I knew you'd never understand. Why should you? I'm the one who screwed up, not you. I figured you'd be better off without me. You *are* better off without me."

Tasha handed her empty glass to her attorney and said, "More."

Thurston stood up, strode into the little kitchen, a study in nonchalance. He returned with a cup of coffee. "Still hot," he said.

Medusa would have been proud of the look Tasha gave him. She reached out and delicately flicked the cup off the saucer. It landed at my feet and rolled. Dark coffee pooled under my wheels.

"You work for me," Tasha said. "Do I have that right, at least? So I tell you to get me a drink, get me a drink. Is that clear?"

"Quite clear," Thurston said. A moment later he returned with a glass of vodka and the requisite pair of ice cubes. "You've a right to get drunk, I suppose. But I doubt that it will help the situation."

"What I do is my own business."

"Of course."

"It was Howard who had the drinking problem. Don't pretend it was *my* fault."

The lawyer responded with a tight smile, but did not return to the couch. Keeping his distance—why risk a stain on those immaculate white trousers? He slipped his hands in his pockets and sauntered over to the writing table. It was in disarray, files scattered. The computer screen still glowed with words, indicating that Fiona had been hard at work when interrupted.

"You know, Howard," he said. "Sorry, I mean Fiona. It wasn't only your marriage you abandoned. There were other family matters. Business matters."

Here it comes, I thought. He can't resist.

"You left the management people in rather an awkward position. Controlling, as you do, the proxy for a sizeable block of shares."

"The proxy goes back to Tasha," Fiona said.

"Yes, but only if you die. When that was questioned it left us with rather a mess."

"I never owned that stock," Fiona said. "Do anything you want with the proxy."

"Oh?" The lawyer said, rocking on his heels. "You won't contest a reversion of proxy to your wife?"

"Of course not," Fiona said.

Tasha, meantime, was retreating into a haze of vodka. Her intention seemed clear enough: to achieve unconsciousness, the sooner the better. Not that she seemed to take any pleasure from the alcohol. It was medication, a way out of her head.

"I have the paperwork here," the lawyer said, lifting up a briefcase that had been buried under Fiona's latest novel. "It's made out in the name of Howard Holton, I hope you don't mind."

Fiona looked surprised. "You want me to sign it now?"

"All biznuss," Tasha commented thickly. "Kill all the lawyers."

"If you don't mind," Thurston said, unsnapping the locks and opening the briefcase. He drew out a single sheet of paper. "It really would help."

"And you'll leave me alone? You'll go away and leave me alone?"

"I will," Thurston said. "Your wife, of course, has her own agenda."

Fiona stood up. She had decided to sign the paper. And I decided to open my big mouth.

3̲1̲

Very neat," I said to Thurston. "Now the board can approve the garage purchase and you'll be a millionaire, just like that."

Fiona dropped back into the chair. "What?"

Tasha's sagging eyelids fluttered. She echoed, "What?"

"It's a sweet deal," I said. "Thurston Breen, Jr., controls Hub City Realty Trust, which in turn holds an option on a piece of property that Sturne Hotels needs to acquire."

"You're mistaken," he said.

I glanced at Tasha. She was sitting bolt upright, her knuckles white as she squeezed the vodka glass.

"I suppose it's all perfectly legal," I said. "You being a lawyer and all."

"I said you're mistaken."

"Right," I said. "You did say that. Was Brant mistaken, too? Is that why you killed him?"

I had to hand it to Thurston Breen, Jr. His cool was impregnable. Never even winced when I mentioned Brant. It was Tasha who looked like she'd been slapped awake.

"Thurston?" she said. "What is he talking about?"

"He's talking nonsense, Tasha. Making it up. You know these writers. And you know very well I was in New York when your brother died."

"Were you?" I said. "Then I guess you've got a twin brother who was seen going into Brant's suite."

I was making that up. You know writers, they're always making things up. Using lies to get at the truth.

"Impossible," he said. Wearily he snapped his briefcase shut. "Come on," he said to Tasha. "We had better leave. I warned you about Hawkins. He's a trouble-maker."

"I'm not ready to leave," she said, sounding as if she'd recovered a measure of sobriety. "Tell me about my brother, Mr. Hawkins. Do you really know who killed him?"

"I think I do."

"Tasha—"

"Shut up, Thurston. Mr. Hawkins wants to tell us a story, don't you, Mr. Hawkins?"

The fire was burning down. Fiona made no attempt to revive it.

"Here's the story, Tasha. I may have some of the details wrong, but the plot isn't terribly complicated, once you understand the motivation. Your attorney was privy to the decision-making process at Sturne International. He was fully aware of all the problems afflicting the new Boston hotel. He took advantage of that knowledge by acquiring an option to purchase a parking garage that fit into the hotel's expansion plans."

Tasha nodded slowly. "I remember something about a garage. They wanted to spend money on it. Lots of money. Had to have parking for a first-class hotel, they said. I never paid much attention."

I grinned at the lawyer and said, "Howard's death must have been a nasty little surprise, hey Thurston? You must have been on pins and needles, waiting for his body to be recovered. If he was dead, fine, Tasha would get his proxy and vote to buy the garage, as the management requested. So you pushed to have him declared dead, even though Tasha and Brant seemed to have their doubts."

"Any good attorney would have insisted on that," he said. "The board was paralyzed. Management was unable to act. *Everybody* wanted him declared dead."

"Except for me," Tasha said, looking pointedly at Fiona. "And Brant. Brant *never* believed it, Howard. He said you'd never let yourself die in such a silly way. Drowned by a fish."

"We really must leave," the lawyer said. "This man Hawkins has poisoned the atmosphere. We'll accomplish nothing by staying."

"Nice try, Thurston," I said.

Fiona, who'd been listening intently, turned to me. "Okay, so he's working an inside deal. But why would he want to kill poor Brant?"

"Care to tell us about that, Thurston?" I said.

"You must be insane. I'm not working any deal and I had nothing whatever to do with Brant dying. And if you persist in these allegations I'll sue for slander."

"Very convincing, but the Homicide Unit has been busy putting the case together. They found fiber evidence on Brant's body. Is that the sweater you were wearing the night he died?"

"I bought this yesterday," he said. "Barneys on Seventh Avenue."

It was clear by now that Thurston was never going to admit to anything. There would be, I sensed, no anguished confessions. I concentrated on reaching Tasha.

"As to why he strangled your brother, I don't suppose we'll ever know his state of mind at the time. My guess is young Thurston never intended to murder anyone when he followed Brant up to Boston. He was trying to locate Howard Holton, probably to get him to sign that release he just showed us. One possibility is that Ted Margolis, the Fitzroy Security investigator, found out about the Hub City Realty Trust. So maybe Brant knew all about Thurston's little scheme." I turned to Thurston. "Is that what the problem was? Did Brant taunt you with that knowledge? Threaten to tell his sister? And when you put your hands around his neck, did he resist? My guess is he didn't, not until it was too late."

The alcohol flush had drained from Tasha's face, leaving the pale blotches of stained porcelain. She propped a cigarette between her lips, reached into her purse for a lighter, had trouble keeping her hand steady. And she never took her eyes off Thurston Breen, Jr.

"Did you really mean to kill him, Thurston?" I said. "Or did you just discover how easy it is to make someone die? Squeeze a little too hard on the vagus nerve and they're gone, just like that. All over in less than thirty seconds, even a big strong boy like Brant could die that way if he didn't fight it right from the start."

Tasha, enunciating carefully, said, "Tell me he's making this up, Thurston."

"Of *course* he's making this up. I was in New York, remember? I met you at the airport. We flew up together."

Tasha closed her eyes. The unlit cigarette trembled in her lips.

"You might beat the fiber evidence," I said. "You probably destroyed whatever you were wearing. You're smart, Thurston, and very resourceful, but you know what's going to sink you? A weak stomach."

Tasha shuddered, as if she'd seen something frightening behind her eyelids.

"You vomited, Thurston, tossed your cookies," I said. "Did it happen right after you realized Brant was dead? Or was it later, after you'd got him hanging from the chandelier? Was it disgust that made you queasy, Thurston, or fear? Maybe a little of each, huh?"

"You're a very sick man, Hawkins. I keep telling you, I was in New York that night."

Tasha opened her eyes and focused on the lawyer.

"Then you won't mind submitting to a blood test," I said. "You won't mind seeing if there's a DNA match with the flecks of blood found in the vomit."

The zinger worked. At the mention of a possible DNA match the mask of confidence dropped, ever so briefly, and a pulse of his fear resonated through the room. In the next instant the mask was back in place, reinforced by an expression of condescending smugness.

"Come along Tasha," he said.

She went into her purse for another cigarette and came out with a pistol. A nice little Llama small-frame with the satin chrome finish.

At first she simply displayed it.

"Remember this, Howard? You gave it to me for my own protection. Insisted I learn how to shoot it. I figured bring it along, scare the hell out of Fiona Darling, this bitch who stole my husband."

"Tasha, put that away," Thurston said.

"Maybe, I don't know, in the back of my mind I intended to shoot her? I figured if Howard was really dead, she killed him somehow, she was responsible and now she was cashing in, stealing his books."

Drunk with a gun, that's what I was thinking. Looking around for something to grab, use it to knock the weapon from her hands.

"I was just thinking about me," Tasha said. "*My* anger, *my* need. Never gave a thought to Brant. Keeping him out, see, out of my head. Wasn't that awful of me? Trying to forget him?"

The lawyer waited. He could have run right then, ducked out of the line of fire, but instead he waited. Convinced, perhaps, that she was about to shoot Fiona. Which would have been fine, from his point of view. A bullet was as good as a signature.

I was sneaking a look up into the rafters, measuring the distance to the fishing gaff that was almost directly overhead. Knock the gaff loose with the fireplace poker, then use the long gaff to hook the gun away from Tasha?

Nah, too complicated. Even slowed by alcohol she'd have plenty of time to turn the gun on me.

"You know what Howard told me?" Tasha said, holding up the gun. Still not pointing it at anyone in particular. "You can never be too close, you want to shoot someone."

Fiona hadn't moved. She looked at the gun with something like longing.

Tasha said: "I do remember meeting you at the airport, Thurston. And you were coming out of Arrivals. You were coming back from Boston. Back from killing Brant."

"Don't be ridiculous," Thurston said.

What happened next was so fast and remains so confused in my mind that I can't say exactly who did what to whom. Tasha stood up, her purse spilling to the floor. Thurston Breen swung his briefcase, let it fly. I never heard the gun discharge. Must have happened when the briefcase collided with her arm, because the gun went flying. Hit the mantel and dropped at Fiona's feet. She looked at it, picked it up, and handed it to me for safekeeping.

"You *bastard!*" Tasha screamed. She tried to slap Thurston but he caught her wrist, fended her off. "You bastard, you killed him."

Good, I thought, hefting the little pistol, now I'm in control.

"Jack?"

Megan hadn't moved from the rocker. She had her hands folded over her stomach. Strangely enough, her fingers were red and shiny.

"Jack?" Meg whispered.

Then she slipped out of the rocking chair and her

hands came away from her stomach and her blood was everywhere, everywhere.

Pain and confusion and the terrible vertigo of fear. I'm not sure what happened to the gun except it was no longer in my hands. Nor do I remember crawling down from my chair and getting on the floor next to Meg. My hands slick with her blood, pressing hard, trying to make it stop.

I remember Fiona saying she would go to the nearest phone and call an ambulance.

I remember Thurston Breen, Jr., with a spot of red on the cuffs of his perfect white trousers. Offering to help but not actually helping.

I remember Tasha with the bottle of vodka, her eyes strangely unfocused, her teeth the color of bones.

I remember being inside the ambulance, and a boy in an EMS uniform who kept saying *I can't find a pulse, where is the pulse?*

I remember Megan Drew dying, fading away under my hands.

hree days later a Nantucket police detective met me in the south lobby of the Massachusetts General Hospital. I got down to the lobby under my own steam, into that place I'll always think of as The Wailing Room. It is a place of pain and anguish and crushed hope, a place of gurneys and wheelchairs and rented crutches. A place where gaunt patients shuffle, dragging IV bottles behind them, a place where parents huddle around sick children who seem already part of another world.

The detective's name was Nelson Metcalf and he had the sad eyes of a man who did not flinch from the truth. "I'm sorry to disturb you, Mr. Hawkins. But I need to get a statement."

"Of course," I said. "Coffee? There's an automat on this floor."

"No thanks," he said. "We've taken statements from both Mr. Breen and Mrs. Holton. They don't agree precisely on the details—two statements rarely do—but the inference seems to be that your wife was shot accidentally. Is that how you remember it?"

I told him what I could. It was like trying to put together images from a shattered mirror—everything was jagged and fragmented. In the end I agreed that Megan was an innocent bystander—no one had intended to shoot her. She was in the wrong place at the wrong time.

"Did you form an impression of Mrs. Holton's intentions?" Metcalf asked. "Was she attempting to shoot Mr. Breen?"

"It happened so fast," I said. "I'm sorry I can't be of more help."

He put away his notebook.

"Boston Homicide has been in touch with us," he said. "They intend to indict Mr. Breen for the murder of Brant Sturne. But I guess you already know that."

"Larry Sheehan was in here yesterday," I said. "Breen won't agree to a blood test. He's going to fight them every step of the way. I hope they find a way to convict the son of a bitch."

"I hope so, too."

Detective Metcalf shook my hand, got up to leave.

"We'll be in touch," he said. "We'll want a statement from your wife, when she's ready."

"Of course."

"I understand it was touch and go."

"She was gone," I said. "Then they put the paddles to her chest and she came back. You happen to see that EMS crew, thank them again for me, please."

"Will do."

When the detective was gone I headed back to the SICU.

It was, strangely enough, the same intensive care unit where I had recovered from surgery. Neurologists poking needles at my unfeeling feet and telling me I would never walk again, better get used to the idea. There was a time when I had hated all doctors, when the look and smell and feel of the hospital was enough to send me into a rage.

You feel differently when someone you love has been brought back to life.

Meg was sleeping again when I got there. She'd been drifting in and out for hours. Exhaustion and stress from the trauma of abdominal surgery. She was pale and weak and her eyes were bruised and she had never looked so beautiful. Just watching her was exhausting.

I dozed off, awakened when someone touched my hand.

"Hi," she said.

"Hello, Meg."

"I feel woozy."

"That's the Demerol. For the pain."

"I'm okay?"

"Better than okay."

She drifted off and I thought she was going to sleep again but this time she seemed to be fighting it.

"What about Fiona?" she asked. "Is she okay, too?"

"Yes," I said. "Fiona is fine."

"Good," she said, and slept.

I knew she would forgive the small lie I'd told her. Truth was, I didn't know that Fiona Darling was fine. After calling the ambulance she had apparently driven the Volkswagen out to the sandy point that overlooks uninhabited Tuckernuck Island. It is a place of desolate beauty and it was there that she left the key in the ignition and walked away. Disappeared.

To me it was like the opening sentence of a new Fiona Darling novel: *They found the battered little car on the last dune facing the sea, but no one could say if those were footprints in the sand, leading to the water's edge—the wind does strange things in Nantucket.*

I'd like to think that Fiona had been planning another escape, that she made it off the island alive, that in another year or so I'd pick up a brand new book by a brand new author and find that familiar voice inside.

Why not? Take it from me, miracles can happen.